On Our Selection

AND

Our New Selection

STEELE RUDD

On Our Selection

AND

Our New Selection

THE COLLECTOR'S LIBRARY OF
AUSTRALIA'S GREAT BOOKS

Published by
TIMES HOUSE

TIMES HOUSE PUBLISHING
61-69 Anzac Parade, Kensington, NSW 2033
Published by arrangement with
Angus & Robertson Publishers

On Our Selection: first published 1899
Our New Selection: first published 1903
Combined edition 1953
Reprinted 1954, 1955, 1959, 1969, 1975, 1980
This Australia's Great Books edition, 1984
Reprinted 1986, 1987
© E. D. Davis. 1899 and 1903
National Library of Australia
Cataloguing-in-publication data.
Rudd, Steele.
    On our selection and Our new selection.
    (Australian literary heritage series).
    First published. Sydney: Bulletin Newspaper Co.
    1899 and 1903.
ISBN 0 85835 711 9

Printed in Singapore
by Toppan Printing Co.

PUBLISHER'S NOTE

In 1895 Steele Rudd contributed to the *Bulletin* the first of the series of sketches which later appeared in book form under the title *On Our Selection*. This book was published in 1899 by the *Bulletin* Newspaper Company, which in 1903 published *Our New Selection*. The copyright was purchased by the N.S.W. Bookstall Company, which in 1909 brought out new editions of both books, *On Our Selection* containing only chapters 1-16 of the original volume, chapters 17-26 and 7 additional chapters being issued under the title *Stocking Our Selection* in the same year. It is the Bookstall Company's edition of *On Our Selection* that is published here.

Serle states that by 1940 about 250,000 copies of *On Our Selection* had been sold.

The illustrations to the original editions of *On Our Selection* and *Our New Selection* are so much part of the stories that a number of them is included in the present edition. The artists here represented, and to whom grateful acknowledgment is due, are Norman Lindsay, G. W. Lambert, Percy Lindsay, Fred Leist, Lionel Lindsay, F. P. Mahony, A. J. Fischer, Alf Vincent, and A. H. Fullwood.

Their varying styles and techniques make the difference in authorship obvious; but no excuse is offered for this lack of homogeneity. These drawings express inimitably the spirit of Steele Rudd's stories and of the period they bring so vividly to life.

PIONEERS OF AUSTRALIA!
TO YOU WHO GAVE OUR COUNTRY BIRTH

To the Memory of You
Whose names, whose giant enterprise, whose deeds of
Fortitude and daring
Were never engraved on tablet or tombstone
To You who strove through the silences of the Bushlands
And made them ours
To You who delved and toiled in loneliness through
The years that have faded away
To You who have no place in the history of our Country
So far as it is yet written
To You who have done MOST for this Land
To You for whom few, in the march of settlement, in the
Turmoil of busy city life, now appear to care
And to You particularly,
GOOD OLD DAD,
This Book
Is most affectionately dedicated.

—STEELE RUDD.

CONTENTS

ON OUR SELECTION

OUR NEW SELECTION

FOREWORD

By W. E. FitzHenry

The *Bulletin* of 6th April 1895, printed at the old office at 24 Pitt Street, Sydney, was, no doubt, considered by the literary staff as just an ordinary run-of-the-press issue. It contained the usual editorials and features of the day, cartoons by Livingston Hopkins and Tom Durkin, drawings by A. J. Fischer, Frank Mahony, and D. H. Souter, verse by E. J. Brady and Arthur H. Adams. There was little, it seemed, to mark it apart from the issue of the week before.

Yet that issue of close on sixty years ago, when J. F. Archibald was editor, James Edmond and Alex Montgomery his associates, and A. G. Stephens had still to start the famous Red Page, is not without a certain importance in the history of Australian literature. For on a back page, in the microscopic type of the period, appeared a short sketch called "Starting the Selection". A simple record of the homely pathos and humour of life on a small Darling Downs selection, it was typical of the stories that were appearing in the *Bulletin* week by week.

The main virtues of *Bulletin* stories of the period—that is, the eighties and nineties—were, to quote a *Southerly* article by Ken Levis, "the general shortness of the stories, objectivity rather than subjectivity, unaffected use of colloquial language, strength of dialogue, preference for stories told in the third person, identification of the writer with the life he deals with, very little of the posing affected by earlier storywriters, avoidance of interpolated comment, greater realism, a political and social interest and awareness, relish of bush yarns and folk-lore, a wry humour, a genuine Australianity."

How well this story begins! Immediately one feels at one with the family in their journey to their new homestead:

> It's twenty years ago now since we settled on the Creek. Twenty years! I remember well the day we came from Stanthorpe, on Jerome's dray—eight of us, and all the things—beds, tubs, a bucket, the two cedar chairs with the pine bottoms and backs that Dad put in them, some pint-pots and old Crib. It was a scorching hot day, too—talk about thirst! At every creek we came to we drank till it stopped running.

Dad did not travel with the family and old Crib. He had gone to the selection some months before, to erect a slabbed house, with shingled roof, and dig a waterhole, and generally get things ready. The property was a "real wilderness—nothing but trees, goannas, dead timber and bears; and the nearest house—Dwyer's—was three miles away. . . . Lonely! It *was* lonely." But Dad thought it was fine land, with valuable timber on it, and gold to be found amongst the rocks on the ridges.

And so the family arrive at Shingle Hut on the creek, with all their goods and chattels and settle down to the heartbreaking business of clearing the selection and getting it under cultivation.

It was thus, in this simple story, that *Bulletin* readers of nearly three generations ago were introduced to the best-known and most lovable family in Australian fiction—the famous Rudd family, the children of the retentive and inventive brain of Arthur Hoey Davis, better known as "Steele Rudd", a young and then unheard-of Queensland writer.

Over the years all Australia was to become familiar with the Rudd family; with Dad (Murtagh Joseph), his wife (Ellen—always Mother in the stories, never Mum); Dan, the prodigal son who was always going off and coming back to loaf on the family and get some local girl into trouble; hard-working, dependable Dave; Joe, an irrepressible young bush scamp, if ever there was one; the twins, and the girls —Kate, Sarah (more often Sal than Sarah) and Norah— and the younger fry, various relatives, Cranky Jack, and the neighbours—the Dwyers, Andersons, Maloneys, and Donovans.

The authenticity of Cranky Jack has often been questioned, but Stewart Howard, reviewing *On Our Selection* in the *Sunday Herald* of 20th September 1953, has this to say about that balmy character:

> To the city mind a Cranky Jack might appear pure invention, a fantastic figure, who could not possibly have any existence outside fiction. But he—or it could have been his twin brother—was alive in 1926; he lived in a hut on the banks of the Shoalhaven working for tucker and an occasional few shillings as Man Friday to the owner of a small, isolated property running a few head of stock, and talking to nobody except his blue cattle dog.

Characters and settings have been borrowed by other writers on many occasions since Dad and Mother and the rest made their début in the middle nineties, but the imitations— they are still going strong to this day—have signally failed to improve on the original. Though created so long ago, the Rudd family still retain their freshness, and as a recorder of their adventures in Shingle Hut, Saddletop, and elsewhere their literary father, Steele Rudd, has had no peer.

Arthur Hoey Davis (the Hoey comes from the name of

a country bookseller) was born at Drayton, near Toowoomba, Queensland, on 14th November 1868. From the
same Queensland district came that redoubtable critic, A.
G. Stephens, the poet George Essex Evans, and J. J. Hilder,
the water-colourist. Steele Rudd was the eighth child in a
family of thirteen. His father, Thomas Davis (originally
Davies), had come from Wales, where he had served an
apprenticeship as a blacksmith and farrier. He is said to have
had a fine tenor voice, and would sing "The Rocky Road to
Dublin" or "The Wind Among the Barley" at the drop of a
hat. It has also been said that Thomas Davis had some en-
gineering knowledge, and that he was with Thomas Mitchell's exploring expedition to the Maranoa and with J. C.
Burnett's survey-party.

Steele Rudd's mother was Mary Green, a colleen from
outside Roscommon, who, had she had her way, would
have made her son a clergyman, like the Rev. Mr Macpherson of the story "The Parson and the Scone", which does
not appear in this edition. Although Steele Rudd does not say
so, the Rev. Mr Macpherson was, no doubt, the parson who
baptized Bartholomew. He certainly married Kate to young
Sandy Taylor. They were fine fellows, those bush parsons
in the old days, but Steele Rudd was not to become one. From
all accounts Mrs Davis must have been a grand woman, one
of the true "women of the West" of the old pioneering days.

Thomas Davis took up a selection at Emu Creek on the
Darling Downs, and there the son was educated at the local
school, which figures in a Steele Rudd book, *On Emu Creek*.
In a letter to A. G. Stephens, dated 27th November 1897,
Steele Rudd said, "When I wasn't watering cows or driving
horses in the plough or hunting kangaroos or bears, I was at
school up to about the age of twelve. I do not know if I was
very bright there, but I remember the school-master telling

me I was the smartest boy in my class. I also remember being the only one in the class."

Winifred Hamilton has said, "Steele Rudd was blessed with no scholarship in the accepted sense of that much misused word, for he had but little book learning; this was more than made up for by an almost unerring capacity for getting to the heart of things through an unadulterated worship for the simple and natural things of life."

After leaving school the boy worked at odd jobs on a station, and at fifteen became a junior stockrider on Pilton station on the Downs. Like Banjo Paterson, he loved horses to the end of his days. In after years he used to tell how, when he was a lad doing the work he loathed, such as yarding sheep and cutting lambs' tails and slashing the Bathurst burr in the summer heat, he was haunted by the dread that he would never get away from the scorching plains. In his own words: "Hammering at the d—— burr all day (and with the fear of snakes) I thought, will there ever be work in the shade or am I doomed to work in this sun with flies and burrs for ever?"

When Steele Rudd was eighteen he became a junior clerk in the office of the Curator of Intestate Estates in Brisbane, and in 1889 was transferred to the Sheriff's office, which is the scene of some amusing incidents in his books *The Dashwoods* and *The Miserable Clerk*.

In his spare time the young man from Emu Creek took up rowing. This led to his contributing a column on rowing to the *Chronicle*, a now long-vanished Brisbane weekly. Finding that he required a pseudonym, he adopted that of "Steele Rudd". The first name was suggested by the name of the English essayist, the second was a shortening of "rudder"; he wanted to bring into his name some part of a boat.

About this time Steele Rudd began to write fiction of a sort, placing a little without payment with a Brisbane weekly. He was advised by an old bachelor where he lodged to "try the *Bulletin*". He did, and got an answer in the "Correspondents" column: "A. H. D., Brisbane: An opium-sodden dream without beginning, middle or end."

That put him off fiction for a couple of years, till he hit on the happy idea of writing his recollections of life on the family selection at Emu Creek. In a magazine article printed forty-five years ago, Steele Rudd said, "Allowing for embroidery, the incidents related in *On Our Selection* are for the most part true. . . . 'Dad' I drew from several sources. He is a triangle or a 'trinity': he is three in one. . . . The only one of the group strictly drawn from life is 'Cranky Jack'."

Writing in the *Bulletin* in 1926, C. H. Winter said, "The Rudds . . . were people 'Steele Rudd' knew intimately and affectionately. Thirty years ago and more, Dad, Mother, the youngsters and their relations were to be found wherever poverty-stricken selectors battled outback. With rare perception and skill Arthur Hoey Davis made them live in print."

Encouraged by J. F. Archibald and A. G. Stephens, he wrote, after his first *Bulletin* success, a herd of selection stories. "They came charging into the office like a mob of wild brumbies," said A. G. Stephens. "There was no stopping them."

"Inspired with confidence," said Steele Rudd, in a magazine article, "I beat out a heavy packet of 'poetry' and directed it to the editor. It was deadly. He dodged it, and warned me to be careful." Some of the poems the *Bulletin* rejected appeared in the *Darling Downs Gazette*.

J. F. Archibald wrote him many letters. "Dear Mr Davis," he wrote in his own hand, "Herewith cheque for

'Fourteen Years Ago', which we'll keep a while for a special occasion. Those selection sketches of yours should be very interesting when collected and published one day." And later Archibald wrote, " 'Lady Comes to Shingle Hut' printed this (coming) week. It is a fine yarn; by such things is your name made. Take my advice, and don't consciously write below your standard."

Some of Archibald's letters to Steele Rudd are preserved in the Mitchell Library, Sydney, as is also an unpublished biography of Steele Rudd by Miss Winifred Hamilton. She was a sub-editor on *Steele Rudd's Magazine*, is an authority on his writings, and knew him personally as few others did.

Towards the end of 1899 the *Bulletin* published in book form *On Our Selection*, a collection of twenty-six of the selection stories. At Archibald's request Steele Rudd enlarged and improved some of the earlier ones. A. G. Stephens, who was head of the *Bulletin's* book-publishing department as well as being its literary editor, steered the book through the press. A fine piece of book production, with its clear type and fawn cloth binding, the 1899 edition has stood up well to the ravages of time. Today the edition commands a fancy price in the second-hand bookshops. It was lavishly illustrated from drawings by A. J. Fischer, A. H. Fullwood, George Lambert, Fred Leist, Frank Mahony, and Alf Vincent. A preliminary announcement stated that the frontispiece was to be by Livingston Hopkins, but one by A. J. Fischer was substituted.

Within four years 20,000 copies had been printed. It afterwards appeared in numerous one-shilling paper-back editions published by the New South Wales Bookstall Company, and by 1940 the number of copies sold had reached 250,000. The later editions of the book issued by the New South Wales Bookstall Company consisted of only sixteen

B

chapters of the original edition. The remaining ten chapters, 17-26, with seven additional chapters, were then published by the same company as *Stocking Our Selection* (1909).

On Our Selection was, according to Winifred Hamilton, pirated by American publishers and Steele Rudd received not one penny. Russian, German, and Scandinavian publishing firms wished to translate it, but Steele Rudd, who was favourable to the project, was foolishly dissuaded by a friend, the argument being that it would be too difficult to check royalty accounts!

Steele Rudd soon had his imitators, among them being Henry Fletcher, with his *Dads Wayback* series, and Sumner Locke, with her *Mum Dawson, Boss* books. Steele Rudd was amazingly tolerant towards his imitators, and when one of them died went out of his way to write an appreciation of the writer for a memorial volume. If one thing made him wild, however, it was a Dad-and-Dave wireless programme that ran some years ago. He objected strongly, too, when he heard the Rudd parents called "Dad and Mum". "It is 'Mother', 'Mother', 'Mother'!" he would shout, flushed in the face. As Cecil Mann said when he was editing the Red Page of the *Bulletin*: "Yet one of those legendary characters he did not create at all—Mum; he always called her Mother, and was fond of her and respected her above all his other people."

In 1912 *On Our Selection*, with incidents from other books, was dramatized and produced by Bert Bailey and his company in Adelaide, Brisbane, Sydney, and Melbourne. The play had an unbroken success in each of the four cities, and remained an Australian stage favourite for many years. The Melbourne *Age*, for instance, reported in September 1912: "In all the imported melodramas, Mr Bailey has done nothing half so humorous as Dad. The audience took Dad to its heart. . . . The scene in which the old man tells of his struggle against drought and disaster rang truly and afforded the strongest piece of acting in the production."

In his book *Towards an Australian Drama* Leslie Rees records that Bert Bailey appeared in other plays by Steele Rudd during the earlier years of the century. *Grandad Rudd* ran at the King's Theatre, Melbourne, and at the Palace and Tivoli, Sydney. There was also *McClure and the Parson*, from another Steele Rudd novel, a fine study of a quiet, uncomplaining, hard-up, self-sacrificing minister with a large family—a type to be found anywhere in the bush in the old days. The selection stories have also been screened in both silent and talking films.

The *Bulletin* followed up the success of *On Our Selection* with the publication in 1903 of *Our New Selection*, a collection of eighteen stories written for its pages, with a story from the *Antipodean* and two previously unpublished stories. In the new book relative prosperity has replaced the struggle at Shingle Hut, and the Rudd family migrate to a larger acreage known as Saddletop. The title-page stated: "This is the book of | Our New Selection | written by Arthur | Hoey Davis, yclept | Steele Rudd—adorned | with many pleasing | Pictures of the Story | by the most notorious Artists." The frontispiece was by Norman Lindsay, and there were illustrations by Norman and Lionel Lindsay, L. H. Booth, and Alf Vincent. The book was dedicated to "The Wives of Australia's Pioneers", and was tastefully bound in decorated cream cloth. By 1907 eleven thousand copies, exhausting the first edition, had been sold. As with the first, the copyright of the second volume was disposed of by the *Bulletin* to the New South Wales Bookstall Company, which published many cheap editions of it over the years.

The New South Wales Bookstall Company afterwards published a long run of selection stories by Steele Rudd in book form, including *Stocking our Selection, Back to Our Selection, Sandy's Selection, Dad in Politics* (which caused a stir; the author was very nearly called to the Bar of the Queensland Legislative Assembly for his satirization of the Government), *From Selection to City, Grandpa's Selection, The Book of Dan*, and others. Most of them, according to Percival Serle, were successful, but there could not have been a great deal of profit for the author from the cheap editions, though Winifred Hamilton has recorded that for *Sandy's Selection* Steele Rudd was paid £500 cash and a royalty on all copies sold outside Australia.

Of the selection books Brian Elliott, in his *Singing to the Cattle*, considers *On Our Selection, Our New Selection*, and *Sandy's Selection* the best. *Sandy's Selection* develops the two earlier selection books. We have some new characters in old guises and old characters in new guises. Sandy and Kate, the story of whose marriage is one of the best chapters in *On Our Selection*, are shown struggling on a fresh selection as much as Dad and Mother struggled in the earlier book; with some variation of incident and detail the theme is the same. The book's characteristic dedication runs thus:

To the memory of the Good Old Times—of the Old Bush Days when we crossed the rolling plains in the dragging, creaking dray—of the Old Homestead where the great trees towered and the long grass reached above our heads; the homestead where the rafters shook to gay bush songs, and we danced and danced the whole night through; the homestead where we toiled and struggled, and hoped and lost; the homestead where our hearts beat free and merriment mocked at adversity—and to you, Old Friends, who shared with me the shade of the apple trees on the plains, in those careless days by mountain, creek and scrub, I fondly dedicate this book.

Dr E. Morris Miller in his *Australian Literature* lists no fewer than twenty-three books by Steele Rudd, including two capable books written towards the end of his life, *The Romance of Runnibede* and *Green Grey Homestead*. Both were departures from the author's usual approach to his characters. In *The Romance of Runnibede*, for instance, an entertaining pioneering novel, vibrant with life and rich in local colour, Steele Rudd handles his characters in a serious mood that is different from the prevailing note of his selection stories.

In a *Bulletin* Red Page article, written shortly after Steele Rudd's death in Brisbane on 11th October 1935, Winifred Hamilton considered that the best work Steele Rudd did is *The Romance of Runnibede*, *Green Grey Homestead*, and a collection of stories published in a periodical, but not published in book form, called *Bush Horses and Bush Horsemen*. In the last named Steele Rudd shows, says Miss Hamilton, "how he had absorbed the ways and haunts of the great mobs, the wild life and mad gallops, the stress and triumphs of long, eerie night rides, the terrors of flooded waters, the heartaches of shifting the stock, the joy of bringing them home again."

Steele Rudd also ventured into magazine-editing and publishing. In 1903, when he had become Under-sheriff, he resigned from the Queensland Public Service, and next year brought out *Rudd's Magazine*, a monthly published at sixpence a copy, which continued for nearly four years, and which was revived under various names during the twenties. It had a longer lease of life than most Australian magazines of the period, but, as was proved even in the case of the substantially backed *Bulletin* monthly, the *Lone Hand*, there was not in those days a sufficiently large public in Australia to support a magazine. According to A. G. Stephens in a 1914 *Bookfellow* article, the *Bulletin* lost £10,000 on its *Lone*

Hand venture. People closely associated with Steele Rudd consider that his losses in the magazine field were proportional.

Steele Rudd attracted some first-class writers and artists to his *Steele Rudd's Xmas Annual* (1917-23), including many of his *Bulletin* contemporaries—Randolph Bedford, Will Ogilvie, David McKee Wright, Edward Dyson, E. S. Sorenson, Arthur Bayldon, and Harold Mercer among the writers; David Low, Ashton Murphy, and Ambrose Dyson among the artists. Ashton Murphy, incidentally, was a Steele Rudd discovery. Steele Rudd introduced him to the *Bulletin* and helped and encouraged him in many ways. Murphy was a bush artist whose quaint, rough-and-ready style appealed to the creator of Dad and Mother.

Steele Rudd has been described as "a tall, ruddy-faced man of mercurial temperament, kind of heart, fiery of temper, an excellent talker and a charming companion". Stephens, commenting on a 1904 photograph of him, said, "He looks what he is, a shrewd, genial native of the bush." The *Bulletin* remembered him at the time of his death as "a tall, gentle man who might, with his close-clipped moustache, have been a retired solicitor or army officer". Miss Hamilton, describing her first meeting with him in 1917, depicts him as being "a tall, well-made, rather ruddy-faced man of middle-age, whose appearance was made distinctive by a pair of very dark, very melancholy-looking eyes".

In the same article Miss Hamilton said:

> One never knew when one was going to quarrel violently with him, or when his companionship was to be a thing of delight. Buoyant, mercurial, irresponsible as a child at times; again vitriolic, intolerant, pouring scorn and contempt on all people and all things. Like all men of strong personality, he was egotistical, and like so many egotists, he was warm-

hearted and sympathetic with a naive simplicity completely disarming. Yet many people have cause to remember his biting satire, of which he was a master, and his blunt condemnation.

The following example of his "biting satire" and "blunt condemnation" is taken from the *Bulletin*. A paragraphist, signing himself "C", had accused Steele Rudd of pirating an incident described in one of his stories, and stated that the incident had been related to him by a friend who "told him the story in course of conversation in a Salvation shelter-shed". Steele Rudd replied:

"C", in last Red Page, impudently asks if I'm prepared to go the whole truth, and nothing but the truth, on the inspiration and authorship of my story "For Life"? Well, I *am*. That yarn, with the exception of names and a touch of "coloring" is true. . . . I defy "C" to bring along the friend who told him the story. . . . Furthermore, I don't believe . . . that such a person ever existed. There are quantities of unreliable paragraphists of the "C" type hanging about; and a shelter-shed is a great place for him. It's his salvation. He should be collected and put on the land, and harrowed in with a steam-roller.

He loved to dress well, and it pained him once when Cecil Mann good-naturedly expressed surprise in an article that the creator of Dad Rudd should have appeared at a literary gathering in a dinner-suit. "How did he expect me to turn up?" he snorted to me at the old *Bulletin* office at 214 George Street. "In moleskin trousers, with a cabbage-tree hat and blucher boots?" I don't think he ever quite forgave Cecil. I know he wrote a three-foolscap-page typed letter to a friend expressing his indignation, and there is a similar letter to another friend among the Steele Rudd manuscripts in the Mitchell Library.

Foreword

As secretary to *Bulletin* editors S. H. Prior and John Webb, I saw a fair deal of Steele Rudd during the nineteen-twenties and early thirties. I was also associated with him in the early days of the Fellowship of Australian Writers, when it was a *fellowship* and a power in the land, in the company of John Le Gay Brereton, Fred Broomfield, Walter Jago, and Roderic Quinn, and was always impressed by his quiet dignity and modesty, and his ever-readiness to help a lame dog over a barbed-wire fence.

He was a constant visitor to the *Bulletin* office during the time he lived in Sydney, and, I might add, a most welcome visitor, for unlike some of the writers and artists who called at the office in those days he caused no trouble and never made an unreasonable demand. His copy was an editor's dream. It was either typed or written in his clear, firm, legible handwriting and required the minimum of sub-editing. He occasionally received an advance payment for un unwritten story, but never let the office down as did some of his fellow writers. He accepted his rejections with philosophical calm and was never heard to question an editorial decision, unlike some others whose every rejection was followed by a stormy outburst. It was a pleasure to do business with him as I had to as liaison officer between the editor and his contributors. S. H. Prior, I knew, held him in very high regard, both as a writer and as a man.

Like Banjo Paterson, Adam Lindsay Gordon, Will Ogilvie, and Harry Morant ("The Breaker"), Steele Rudd had a great love for horses, and for twenty-five years was one of Queensland's leading polo players. His reputation in the saddle was always one of extraordinary erectness, no matter what the speed or pace—which reminds me that he once wrote a poem about a polo match. The poem appeared in the *Darling Downs Gazette*, and concerned a polo match between Brisbane and Toowoomba, in which the Brisbane team lost, eight goals to nil. Titled "McNade of Hodgson's Run" it began:

A team of Brisbane polo men came to Toowoomba town,
To meet the pick of the polo kings and take Toowoomba down.

Asked once by the *Bulletin* why he was not writing as much as usual, he replied, "Am going strong on polo, developing a dangerous passion for the sport. And when there is a horse to belt and bullock about, Dad and Dave and the selection and the 'roo and the Red Page can all slide." And something of his attitude towards life was expressed in the concluding paragraph of the letter: "Lord, give us plenty *sport*, and keep us full and merry and never mind the money! Poor Lawson and that Hard-up Confession of his nearly made me sad. Would like to have him in a spring-cart with the winkers off the horse, just to shake the funeral services out of his bright head."

As an old admirer of Steele Rudd—it must be thirty-five years since I first read his selection stories in the old Book-stall paper-backs—I am delighted to write this somewhat rambling foreword for the Angus and Robertson edition of *On Our Selection* and *Our New Selection* in one volume.

It has always been a mystery to me why that far-seeing and enterprising publisher, George Robertson, one of the two founders of Angus and Robertson, allowed A. C. Row-landson, of the New South Wales Bookstall Company, to get in ahead of him when the *Bulletin* disposed its selection stories copyright. Anyhow, I am glad that at last this, the richest comedy-chronicle in Australian literature, is in the hands of the firm which has done so much to foster Austra-lian writing, much as I regret that the exigencies of pub-lishing economics have prevented the publication of the two books in their entirety within the one cover.

As has been remarked often, the Rudd family belong almost to our folk-lore. Over the last half-century the original characters have been burlesqued and distorted by others. But no counterfeit presentation has the same charm, the same large-as-life authenticity and sympathetic treatment that belong to the author's original.

One is pleased to meet Dad again—Dad and his struggles with crops, his troubles with the storekeepers, his expedients for raising the wind, his anxieties and his unquenchable hopes. I have always admired the way in which Dad could always be depended upon to come to the rescue whenever a crisis occurred. One such crisis happens in the story "When the Wolf Was at the Door", when the family was without tea, "so Dad showed Mother how to make a new kind. He roasted a slice of bread on the fire till it was like a black coal, then poured the boiling water over it and let it draw well. Dad said it had a capital flavour—*he* liked it!"

And Mother! How many times had she to shake the flour-bag to get enough to make scones for the morning's break-fast, or to send Sal across to the Andersons for a cup of sugar? And the times when there wasn't even enough cotton to mend the children's bits of clothes? Yet, although the family was much oftener in money-trouble than out of it, health and light hearts they shared as a matter of course.

One always remembered Joe with glee. "Joe was a natura-list. He spent a lot of time, time that Dad considered should have been employed cutting burr or digging potatoes, in ear-marking bears or bandicoots, and catching goannas and letting them go without their tails, or coupled in pairs with pieces of greenhide. The paddock was full of goannas in harness and slit-eared bears. They belonged to Joe." Of course Joe, like the rest of them, grew up—"broad-shoul-dered, sturdy, full-faced and droll—he was our own comedian, entertained us often, and gave us pains in the side by taking people off".

One's heart always warmed to Sal, though Sal never wore stockings, except, perhaps, to a funeral—for "the Creek wasn't much of a place for sport"—she was infinitely better off than Miss Ribbone, the anaemic schoolmistress, who couldn't, or wouldn't, eat pumpkin, the staple diet at Shingle Creek. Changed circumstances, however, made a new girl of Sal. When the family moved to Saddletop she had an abundance of leisure time and "revelled in reading the *Family Herald* and other intellectual papers; took a keen interest in fashions and studied etiquette hard".

Then there was Kate. When Kate was married everyone thought she looked very nice—"And orange blossoms! You'd have thought she was an orange-tree with a new bed-curtain thrown over it."

Reading *On Our Selection* and *Our New Selection* again, a dozen or more stories that excited our attention in the past come to mind. There is the inimitable story of "The Parson and the Scone" (which one would like to see restored in some future edition), and the hilarious story of Dave's snake-bite and the telling of the training of Old Bess to win the Overhaul Handicap. There is the homely pathos of "Our First Harvest" and "When the Wolf Was at the Door"—that was when Dan first left home—and the simple artistry of that little classic, "The Night We Watched for Walla-bies", and the fun and swing and spirit of "Kate's Wedding" and "A Surprise Party"—real Australian stories.

More than fifty years ago the *Bulletin* said: "In Arthur Davis, indeed, we have the first Australian humorist who has risen to the eminence of a Book. He takes as a writer of humorous prose the place which A. B. Paterson holds as a writer of humorous verse, and is even more racy of the soil.

Foreword

Lawson's is a saturnine humor; but Paterson and Davis bubble with spontaneous fun."

Present-day Australian readers now have the opportunity long denied them of appreciating the hearty fun and honest laughter which moved their fathers and grandfathers to read Steele Rudd's stories as fast as they appeared in print in the columns of the *Bulletin*. Every reader, I feel sure, will find something refreshing, entertaining and vastly amusing in Steele Rudd's inimitable, original prose.

On Our Selection

Chapter I

STARTING THE SELECTION

IT's twenty years ago now since we settled on the Creek. Twenty years! I remember well the day we came from Stanthorpe, on Jerome's dray—eight of us, and all the things—beds, tubs, a bucket, the two cedar chairs with the pine bottoms and backs that Dad put in them, some pint-pots and old Crib. It was a scorching hot day, too—talk about thirst! At every creek we came to we drank till it stopped running.

Dad didn't travel up with us: he had gone some months before, to put up the house and dig the water-hole. It was a slabbed house, with shingled roof, and space enough for two rooms, but the partition wasn't up. The floor was earth, but Dad had a mixture of sand and fresh cow-dung with which he used to keep it level. About once every month he would put it on, and everyone had to keep outside that day till it was dry. There were no locks on the doors. Pegs were put in to keep them fast at night, and the slabs were not very close together, for we could easily see anybody coming on horseback by looking through them. Joe and I used to play at counting the stars through the cracks in the roof.

The day after we arrived Dad took Mother and us out to see the paddock and the flat on the other side of the gully that he was going to clear for cultivation. There was no fence round the paddock, but he pointed out on a tree the surveyor's marks showing the boundary of our ground. It must have been fine land, the way Dad talked about it. There was very valuable timber on it, too, so he said; and he showed us a place among some rocks on a ridge where he was sure gold would be found, but we weren't to say anything about it. Joe and I went back that evening and turned over every stone on the ridge, but we didn't find any gold.

No mistake, it was a real wilderness—nothing but trees, goannas, dead timber, and bears; and the nearest house, Dwyer's, was three miles away. I often wonder how the women stood it the first few years, and I can remember how Mother, when she was alone, used to sit on a log where the lane is now and cry for hours. Lonely! It *was* lonely.

Dad soon talked about clearing a couple of acres and putting in corn—all of us did, in fact—till the work commenced. It was a delightful topic before we started, but in two weeks the clusters of fires that illuminated the whooping bush in the night, and the crash upon crash of the big trees as they fell, had lost all their poetry.

We toiled and toiled clearing those four acres, where the haystacks are now standing, till every tree and sapling that had grown there was down. We thought then the worst was over—but how little we knew of clearing land! Dad was never tired of calculating and telling us how much the crop would fetch if the ground could only be got ready in time to put it in; so we laboured the harder.

With our combined male and female forces and the aid of a sapling lever we rolled the thundering big logs together in the face of hell's own fires; and when there were no logs to roll it was tramp, tramp the day through, gathering arm-

4

fuls of sticks, while the clothes clung to our backs with a muddy perspiration. Sometimes Dan and Dave would sit in the shade beside the billy of water and gaze at the small patch that had taken so long to do, then they would turn hopelessly to what was before them and ask Dad (who would never take a spell) what was the use of thinking of ever getting such a place cleared. And when Dave wanted to know why Dad didn't take up a place on the plain, where there were no trees to grub and plenty of water, Dad would cough as if something was sticking in his throat, and then curse terribly about the squatters and political jobbery. He would soon cool down, though, and get hopeful again.

"Look at the Dwyers," he'd say. "From ten acres of wheat they got seventy pounds last year, besides feed for the fowls. They've got corn in now, and there's only the two of them."

It wasn't only burning off! Whenever there was a short drought the waterhole was sure to run dry. Then we had to take turns to carry water from the springs—about two miles. We had no draught-horse, and even if we had had one there was neither water-cask, trolly, nor dray. So we humped it—and talk about a drag! By the time you returned, if you hadn't drained the bucket, in spite of the big drink you'd take before leaving the springs, more than half would certainly be spilt through the vessel bumping against your leg every time you stumbled in the long grass. Somehow, none of us liked carrying water. We would sooner keep the fires going all day without dinner than do a trip to the springs.

One hot, thirsty day it was Joe's turn with the bucket, and he managed to get back without spilling very much. We were all pleased because there was enough left after the tea had been made to give us each a drink. Dinner was nearly over. Dan had finished and was taking it easy on the sofa when Joe said, "I say, Dad, what's a nater-dog like?"

C

Dad told him. "Yellow, sharp ears and bushy tail."

"Those muster bin some then that I seen—I don't know 'bout the bushy tail—all the hair had comed off."

"Where'd y' see them, Joe?" we asked.

"Down 'n the springs floating about—dead."

Then everyone seemed to think hard and look at the tea. *I* didn't want any more. Dan jumped off the sofa and went outside; and Dad looked after Mother.

At last the four acres—except for the biggest of the ironbark-trees and about fifty stumps—were pretty well cleared. Then came a problem that couldn't be worked out on a draught-board. I have already said that we hadn't any draught-horses. Indeed, the only thing on the selection like a horse was an old "tuppy" mare that Dad used to straddle. The date of her foaling went farther back than Dad's, I believe, and she was shaped something like an alderman. We found her one day in about eighteen inches of mud, with both eyes picked out by the crows, and her hide bearing evidence that a feathery tribe had made a roost of her carcass. Plainly, there was no chance of breaking up the ground with her help. And we had no plough. How, then, was the corn to be put in? That was the question.

Dan and Dave sat outside in the corner of the chimney, both scratching the ground with a chip and not saying anything. Dad and Mother sat inside talking it over. Sometimes Dad would get up and walk round the room shaking his head, then he would kick old Crib for lying under the table. At last Mother struck something which brightened him up, and he called Dave.

"Catch Topsy and—" he paused because he remembered the old mare was dead.

"Run over and ask Mr Dwyer to lend me three hoes."

Dave went. Dwyer lent the hoes, and the problem was solved. That was how we started.

Chapter II

OUR FIRST HARVEST

I F there is anything worse than burr-cutting or breaking
stones, it's putting corn in with a hoe.

We had just finished. The girls were sowing the last
of the grain when Fred Dwyer appeared on the scene. Dad
stopped and talked with him while we (Dan, Dave and
myself) sat on our hoe-handles, like kangaroos on their tails,
and killed flies. Terrible were the flies, particularly when
you had sore legs or the blight.

Dwyer was a big man with long, brown arms and red,
bushy whiskers.

"You must find it slow work with a hoe," he said.

"Well—yes—pretty," replied Dad (just as if he wasn't quite sure).

After a while Dwyer walked over the "cultivation", and looked at it hard, then scraped a hole with the heel of his boot, spat, and said he didn't think the corn would ever come up. Dan slid off his perch at this, and Dave let the flies eat his leg nearly off without seeming to feel it; but Dad argued it out.

"Orright, orright," said Dwyer. "I hope it *do*."

Then Dad went on to speak of places he knew of where they preferred hoes to a plough for putting corn in with, but Dwyer only laughed and shook his head.

"Damn him!" Dad muttered, when he had gone. "What rot! *Won't come up!*"

Dan, who was still thinking hard, at last straightened himself up and said *he* didn't think it was any use either. Then Dad lost his temper.

"No *use*?" he yelled. "You whelp, what do you know about it?"

Dan answered quietly, "On'y this, that it's nothing but tomfoolery, this hoe business."

"How would you do it then?" Dad roared, and Dan hung his head and tried to button his buttonless shirt wristband while he thought.

"With a plough," he answered.

Something in Dad's throat prevented him saying what he wished, so he rushed at Dan with the hoe. But he was too slow.

Dan slept outside that night.

No sooner was the grain sown than it rained. How it rained! For weeks! And in the midst of it all the corn came up—every grain—and proved Dwyer a bad prophet. Dad

8

was in high spirits and promised each of us something—new boots all round.

The corn continued to grow—so did our hopes, but a lot faster. Pulling the suckers and "heeling it up" with hoes was child's play—we liked it. Our thoughts were all on the boots. It was months since we had pulled on a pair. Every night, in bed, we decided twenty times over whether they would be lace-ups or bluchers, and Dave had a bottle of goanna oil ready to keep his soft with.

Dad now talked of going up country—"to keep the wolf from the door", as Mother put it—while the four acres of corn ripened. He went, and returned on the day Tom and Bill were born—twins. Maybe his absence did keep the wolf from the door, but it didn't keep the dingoes from the fowl-house!

Once the corn ripened it didn't take long to pull it, but Dad had to put on his considering-cap when we came to the question of getting it in. To hump it in bags seemed inevitable till Dwyer asked Dad to give him a hand to put up a milking-yard. Then Dad's chance came, and he seized it.

Dwyer, in return for Dad's labour, carted in the corn and took it to the railway station when it was shelled. Yes, *when* it was shelled! We had to shell it with our hands, and what a time we had! For the first half-hour we didn't mind it at all, and shelled cob after cob as though we liked it. But next day, talk about blisters! We couldn't close our hands for them, and our faces had to go without a wash for a fortnight.

Fifteen bags we got off the four acres, and the storekeeper undertook to sell it. Corn was then at twelve shillings and fourteen shillings per bushel, and Dad expected a big cheque.

Every day for nearly three weeks he trudged over to the store (five miles) and I went with him. Each time the storekeeper would shake his head and say, "No word yet."

Dad couldn't understand. At last word did come. The storekeeper was busy serving a customer when we went in, so he told Dad to "hold on a bit".

Dad felt very pleased—so did I.

The customer left. The storekeeper looked at Dad and twirled a piece of string round his first finger, then said, "Twelve pounds your corn cleared, Mr Rudd, but, of course"—going to a desk—"there's that account of yours which I have credited with the amount of the cheque. That brings it down now to just three pounds, as you will see by the account."

Dad was speechless, and looked sick.

He went home and sat on a block and stared into the fire with his chin resting in his hands, till Mother laid her hand upon his shoulder and asked him kindly what was the matter. Then he drew the storekeeper's bill from his pocket, and handed it to her, and she too sat down and gazed into the fire.

That was our first harvest.

Chapter III

BEFORE WE GOT THE DEEDS

OUR selection adjoined a sheep-run on the Darling Downs, and boasted of few and scant improvements, though things had gradually got a little better than when we started. A verandaless four-roomed slab hut now standing out from a forest of box-trees, a stock-yard, and six acres under barley, were the only evidence of settlement. A few horses—not ours—sometimes grazed about and occasionally a mob of cattle—also not ours. Cows with young calves, steers, and an old bull or two, would stroll round, chew the best legs of any trousers that might be hanging on the log reserved as a clothes-line, then leave in the night and be seen no more for months—some of them never.

And yet we were always out of meat.

Dad was up the country earning a few pounds—the corn drove him up when it didn't bring what he expected. All we got out of it was a bag of flour. I don't know what the store-keeper got. Before he left we put in the barley. Somehow Dad didn't believe in sowing any more crops; he seemed to lose heart. But Mother talked it over with him and, when reminded that he would soon be entitled to the deeds, he brightened up again and worked. How he worked!

We had no plough, so old Anderson turned over the six acres for us, and Dad gave him a pound an acre—at least he was to send him the first six pounds got up country. Dad sowed the seed, then he, Dan and Dave yoked themselves to a large dry bramble each and harrowed it in. From the way they sweated it must have been hard work. Sometimes they would sit down in the middle of the paddock and spell, but Dad would say something about getting the deeds and they'd start again.

A cockatoo-fence was round the barley; and wire-posts, a long distance apart, round the grass-paddock. We were to get the wire to put in when Dad sent the money, and to apply for the deeds when he came back. Things would be different then, according to Dad, and the farm would be worked properly. We would break up fifty acres, build a barn, buy a reaper, ploughs, and a cornsheller, and get cows and good horses. Meanwhile, if we (Dan, Dave and I) minded the barley he was sure there'd be something got out of it.

Dad had been away about six weeks. Travellers were passing by every day, and there wasn't one that didn't want a little of something or other. Mother used to ask them if they had met Dad. None ever did until an old grey man came along and said he knew Dad well—he had camped with him one night and shared a damper. Mother was very pleased and brought him in. We had a kangaroo-rat (stewed) for dinner that day. The girls didn't want to put it on the table at first, but Mother said he wouldn't know what it was. The traveller was very hungry and liked it, and when passing his plate the second time for more he said it wasn't often *he* got any poultry.

He tramped on again, and the girls were very glad he didn't know it was a rat. But Dave wasn't so sure that he didn't know a rat from a rooster, and reckoned he hadn't met Dad at all.

The seventh week Dad came back. He arrived at night, and the lot of us had to get up to find the hammer to knock the peg out of the door and let him in. He brought home three pounds—not enough to get the wire with, but he also brought a horse and saddle. He didn't say if he had bought them. It was a bay mare, a grand animal for a journey—so Dad said—and only wanted condition. Emelina, he called her. No mistake, she was a quiet mare! We put her where there was good feed, but she wasn't one that fattened on grass. Birds took kindly to her—crows mostly—and she couldn't go anywhere but a flock of them accompanied her. Even when Dad used to ride her (Dan or Dave never rode her) they used to follow, and would fly on ahead to wait in a tree and caw when he was passing beneath.

One morning when Dan was digging potatoes for dinner —splendid potatoes they were, too, Dad said; he had only once tasted sweeter ones, but they were grown in a cemetery —he found the kangaroos had been in the barley. We knew what *that* meant, and that night made fires round it, thinking to frighten them off; but mobs of them were in at daybreak. Dad swore from the house at hem, but they took no notice, and when he ran down they just hopped over the fence and sat looking at him. Poor Dad! I don't know if he was knocked up or if he didn't know any more, but he stopped swearing and sat on a stump looking at a patch of barley they had destroyed, shaking his head. Perhaps he was wishing that he had a dog. We did have one until he got a bait. Old Crib. He was lying under the table at supper-time when he took the first fit, and what a fright we got! He must have reared before stiffening out, because he capsized the table into Mother's lap, and everything on it smashed except the tin plates and the pints. The lamp fell on Dad, too, and the melted fat scalded his arm. Dad dragged Crib out and cut off his tail and ears, but he might as well have taken off his head.

Dad stood with his back to the fire while Mother was putting a stitch in his trousers. "There's nothing for it but to watch them at night," he was saying, when old Anderson appeared and asked if he could have those few pounds. Dad asked Mother if she had any money in the house. Of course she hadn't. Then he told Anderson he would let him have it when he got the deeds. Anderson left, and Dad sat on the edge of the sofa and seemed to be counting the grains on a corn-cob that he lifted from the floor, while Mother sat looking at a kangaroo-tail on the table and didn't notice the cat drag it off.

At last Dad said, "Ah, well, it won't be long now, Ellen, before we have the deeds."

We took it in turns to watch the barley. Dan and the two girls watched the first half of the night, and Dad, Dave and I the second. Dad always slept in his clothes, and he used to think some nights that the others came in before time. It was terrible going out, half awake, to tramp round that paddock from fire to fire, from hour to hour, shouting and yelling. And how we used to long for daybreak! Whenever we sat down quietly together for a few minutes we would hear the dull *thud! thud! thud!*—the kangaroo's footstep.

At last we each carried a kerosene tin, slung like a kettle-drum, and belted it with a waddy—Dad's idea. He himself manipulated an old bell that he had found on a bullock's grave, and made a splendid noise with it.

It was a hard struggle, but we succeeded in saving the bulk of the barley, and cut it down with a scythe and three reaping-hooks. The girls helped to bind it, and Jimmy Mulcahy carted it in return for three days' binding Dad put in for him. The stack wasn't built twenty-four hours when a score of somebody's crawling cattle ate their way up to their tails in it. We took the hint and put a sapling fence round it.

Again Dad decided to go up country for a while. He caught Emelina after breakfast, rolled up a blanket, told us to watch the stack, and started. The crows followed.

We were having dinner. Dave said, "Listen!" We listened, and it seemed as though all the crows and other feathered demons of the wide bush were engaged in a mighty scrimmage. "Dad's back!" Dan said, and rushed out in the lead of a stampede.

Emelina was back, anyway, with the swag on, but Dad wasn't. We caught her, and Dave pointed to white spots all over the saddle, and said, "Hanged if they haven't been ridin' her!"—meaning the crows.

Mother got anxious, and sent Dan to see what had happened. Dan found Dad, with his shirt off, at a pub on the main road, wanting to fight the publican for a hundred pounds, but couldn't persuade him to come home. Two men brought him home that night on a sheep-hurdle, and he gave up the idea of going away.

After all, the barley turned out well. There was a good price that year, and we were able to run two wires round the paddock.

One day a bulky government letter came. Dad looked surprised and pleased, and how his hand trembled as he broke the seal! "The deeds!" he said, and all of us gathered round to look at them. Dave thought they were like the inside of a bear-skin covered with writing.

Dad said he would ride to town at once, and went for Emelina.

"Couldn't y' find her, Dad?" Dan said, seeing him return without the mare.

Dad cleared his throat, but didn't answer. Mother asked him.

"Yes, I *found* her," he said slowly, "*dead.*"

The crows had got her at last.

He wrapped the deeds in a piece of rag and walked.

There was nothing, scarcely, that he didn't send out from town, and Jimmy Mulcahy and old Anderson many and many times after that borrowed our dray.

Dad regularly cursed the deeds every mail-day, and wished to Heaven he had never got them.

Chapter IV

WHEN THE WOLF WAS AT THE DOOR

THERE had been a long stretch of dry weather, and we were cleaning out the waterhole. Dad was down the hole shovelling up the dirt; Joe squatted on the brink catching flies and letting them go again without their wings, a favourite amusement of his; while Dan and Dave cut a drain to turn the water that ran off the ridge into the hole—when it rained. Dad was feeling dry, and told Joe to fetch him a drink.

Joe said, "See first if this cove can fly with only one wing." Then he went, but returned and said, "There's no water in the bucket—Mother used the last drop to boil the punkins," and renewed the flycatching. Dad tried to spit, and was going to say something when Mother, half-way between the house and the waterhole, cried out that the grass-paddock was all on fire. "So it is, Dad," said Joe, slowly but surely dragging the head off a fly with finger and thumb.

Dad scrambled out of the hole and looked. "Good God!" was all he said. How he ran! All of us rushed after him except Joe—he couldn't run very well, because the day before he had ridden fifteen miles on a poor horse, bare-back. When near the fire Dad stopped running to break a green bush. He hit upon a tough one. Dad was in a hurry. The bush wasn't. Dad swore and tugged with all his might. Then the bush broke and Dad fell heavily upon his back and swore again.

To save the cockatoo-fence that was round the cultivation was what was troubling Dad. Right and left we fought the fire with boughs. Hot! It was hellish hot! Whenever there was a lull in the wind we worked. Like a windmill Dad's bough moved—and how he rushed for another when that was used up! Once we had the fire almost under control, but the wind rose again, and away went the flames higher and faster than ever.

"It's no use," said Dad at last, placing his hand on his head and throwing down his bough. We did the same, then stood and watched the fence go. After supper we went out again and saw it still burning. Joe asked Dad if he didn't think it was a splendid sight. Dad didn't answer him; he didn't seem conversational that night.

We decided to put the fence up again. Dan had sharpened the axe with a broken file, and he and Dad were about to start when Mother asked them what was to be done about flour. She said she had shaken the bag to get enough to make scones for that morning's breakfast, and unless some was got somewhere there would be no bread for dinner.

Dad reflected, while Dan felt the edge on the axe with his thumb.

Dad said, "Won't Mrs Dwyer let you have a dishful until we get some?"

"No," Mother answered, "I can't ask her until we send back what we owe them."

Dad reflected again. "The Andersons, then?" he said.

Mother shook her head and asked what good there was in sending to them when they, only that morning, had sent to her for some.

"Well, we must do the best we can at present," Dad answered, "and I'll go to the store this evening and see what is to be done."

Putting the fence up again, in the hurry that Dad was in, was the very devil! He felled the saplings—and such saplings —*trees* many of them were—while we, all of a muck of sweat, dragged them into line. Dad worked like a horse himself and expected us to do the same. "Never mind staring about you," he'd say, if he caught us looking at the sun to see if it were coming dinner-time. "There's no time to lose if we want to get the fence up and crop in."

Dan worked nearly as hard as Dad until he dropped the butt-end of a heavy sapling on his foot, which made him hop about on one leg and say that he was sick and tired of the dashed fence. Then he argued with Dad, and declared that it would be far better to put a wire fence up at once, and be done with it, instead of wasting time over a thing that would only be burnt down again. "How long," he said, "will it take to get the posts? Not a week", and he hit the ground disgustedly with a piece of stick he had in his hand.

"Confound it!" Dad said. "Haven't you got any sense, boy? What earthly use would a wire fence be without any wire in it?"

Then we knocked off and went to dinner.

No one appeared in any humour to talk at the table.

Mother sat silently at the end and poured out the tea while Dad, at the head, served the pumpkin and divided what cold meat there was. Mother wouldn't have any meat—one of us would have to go without if she had taken any.

I don't know if it was on account of Dan's arguing with him, or if it was because there was no bread for dinner, that Dad was in a bad temper. Anyway, he swore at Joe for coming to the table with dirty hands. Joe cried and said that he couldn't wash them when Dave, as soon as he had washed his, had thrown the water out. Then Dad scowled at Dave, and Joe passed his plate along for more pumpkin.

Dinner was almost over when Dan, still looking hungry, grinned and asked Dave if he wasn't going to have some *bread*. Whereupon Dad jumped up in a tearing passion. "Damn your insolence!" he said to Dan. "Make a jest of it, would you?"

"Who's jestin'?" Dan answered and grinned again.

"Go!" said Dad furiously, pointing to the door. "Leave my roof, you thankless dog!"

Dan went that night.

It was only when Dad promised faithfully to reduce his account within two months that the storekeeper let us have another bag of flour on credit. And what a change that bag of flour wrought! How cheerful the place became all at once! And how enthusiastically Dad spoke of the farm and the prospects of the coming season!

Four months had gone by. The fence had been up some time and ten acres of wheat had been put in; but there had been no rain, and not a grain had come up, or was likely to.

Nothing had been heard of Dan since his departure. Dad spoke about him to Mother. "The scamp," he said, "to leave me just when I wanted help. After all the years I've slaved to feed him and clothe him, see what thanks I get! But, mark my word, he'll be glad to come back yet." But Mother would never say anything against Dan.

The weather continued dry. The wheat didn't come up, and Dad became despondent again.

The storekeeper called every week and reminded Dad of his promise. "I would give it to you willingly," Dad would say, "if I had it, Mr Rice, but what can I do? You *can't* knock blood out of a stone."

We ran short of tea, and Dad thought to buy more with the money Anderson owed him for some fencing he had done. But when he asked for it, Anderson was very sorry he hadn't got it just then, but promised to let him have it as soon as he could sell his chaff. When Mother heard Anderson couldn't pay, she *did* cry, and said there wasn't a bit of sugar in the house, or enough cotton to mend the children's bits of clothes.

We couldn't very well go without tea, so Dad showed Mother how to make a new kind. He roasted a slice of bread on the fire till it was like a black coal, then poured the boiling water over it and let it draw well. Dad said it had a capital flavour—*he* liked it.

Dave's only pair of pants were pretty well worn off him; Joe hadn't a decent coat for Sunday; Dad himself wore a pair of boots with soles tied on with wire; and Mother fell sick. Dad did all he could—waited on her, and talked hopefully of the fortune which would come to us some day—but once, when talking to Dave, he broke down, and said he didn't, in the name of Almighty God, know what he would do. Dave couldn't say anything—he moped about, too, and home somehow didn't seem like home at all.

When Mother was sick and Dad's time was mostly taken up nursing her, when there was hardly anything in the house, when, in fact, the wolf was at the very door, Dan came home

D

with a pocket full of money and swag full of greasy clothes.
How Dad shook him by the hand and welcomed him back!
And how Dan talked of tallies, belly-wool, and ringers, and
implored Dad, over and over again, to go shearing, or rolling
up, or branding—*anything* rather than work and starve on
the selection.

But Dad stayed on the farm.

Chapter V

THE NIGHT WE WATCHED FOR WALLABIES

I T had been a bleak July day, and as night came on a bitter westerly howled through the trees. Cold! Wasn't it cold! The pigs in the sty, hungry and half fed—we wanted for ourselves the few pumpkins that had survived the drought—fought savagely with each other for shelter, and squealed all the time like—well, like pigs. The cows and calves left the place to seek shelter away in the mountains, while the draught-horses, their hair standing up like barbed wire, leant sadly over the fence and gazed up at the green lucerne. Joe went about shivering in an old coat of Dad's with only one sleeve to it—a calf had fancied the other one day that Dad hung it on a post as a mark to go by while ploughing.

"My! It'll be a stinger tonight," Dad remarked to Mrs Brown, who sat, cold-looking, on the sofa, as he staggered inside with an immense log for the fire. A log! nearer a whole tree! But wood was nothing in Dad's eyes.

Mrs Brown had been at our place five or six days. Old Brown called occasionally to see her, so we knew they couldn't have quarrelled. Sometimes she did a little house-work, but more often she didn't. We talked it over together, but couldn't make it out. Joe asked Mother, but she had no idea—so she said. We were full up, as Dave put it, of Mrs Brown, and wished her out of the place. She had taken to ordering us about, as though she had something to do with us.

After supper we sat round the fire—as near to it as we could without burning ourselves—Mrs Brown and all, and listened to the wind whistling outside. Ah, it was pleasant beside the fire listening to the wind! When Dad had warmed himself back and front he turned to us and said, "Now, boys, we must go directly and light some fires and keep those wallabies back."

That was a shock to us, and we looked at him to see if he were really in earnest. He was, and as serious as a judge.

"*Tonight!*" Dave answered surprisedly. "Why tonight any more than last night or the night before? Thought you had decided to let them rip?"

"Yes, but we might as well keep them off a bit longer."

"But there's no wheat there for them to get now. So what's the good of watching them? There's no sense in *that*."

Dad was immovable.

"Anyway," whined Joe, "*I'm* not going—not a night like this—not when I ain't got boots."

That vexed Dad. "Hold your tongue, sir!" he said. "You'll do as you're told."

But Dave hadn't finished. "I've been following that harrow since sunrise this morning," he said, "and now you want me to go chasing wallabies about in the dark, a night like this, and for nothing else but to keep them from eating the ground. It's always the way here, the more you do the more you're wanted to do", and he commenced to cry. Mrs Brown had something to say. *She* agreed with Dad and thought we ought to go, as the wheat might spring up again.

"Pshah!" Dave blurted out between his sobs, while we thought of telling her to shut her mouth.

Slowly and reluctantly we left that roaring fireside to accompany Dad that bitter night. It *was* a night! Dark as pitch, silent, forlorn and forbidding, and colder than the busiest morgue. And just to keep wallabies from eating

nothing! They had eaten all the wheat—every blade of it—
and the grass as well. What they would start on next—ourselves or the cart-harness—wasn't quite clear.

We stumbled along in the dark, one behind the other, with
our hands stuffed into our trousers. Dad was in the lead, and
poor Joe, bare-shinned and bootless, in the rear. Now and
again he tramped on a Bathurst burr, and in sitting down to
extract the prickle would receive a cluster of them elsewhere.
When he escaped the burr it was only to knock his shin
against a log or leave a toe-nail or two clinging to a stone.
Joe howled, but the wind howled louder, and blew and blew.

Dave in pausing to wait for Joe, would mutter, "To *hell*
with everything! Whatever he wants, bringing us out a night
like this, I'm damned if *I* know!"

Dad couldn't see very well in the dark, and on this night
couldn't see at all, so he walked up against one of the old
draught-horses that had fallen asleep gazing at the lucerne.
And what a fright they both got! The old horse took it
worse than Dad—who only tumbled down—for he plunged
as though the Devil had grabbed him, and fell over the fence,
twisting every leg he had in the wires. How the brute
struggled! We stood and listened to him. After kicking
panels of the fence down and smashing every wire in it, he
got loose and made off, taking most of it with him.

"That's one wallaby on the wheat, anyway," Dave muttered, and we giggled. *We* understood Dave, but Dad didn't
open his mouth.

We lost no time lighting the fires. Then we walked
through the "wheat" and wallabies. May Satan reprove me
if I exaggerate their number by one solitary pair of ears, but
from the row and scatter they made there were a million.

Dad told Joe, at last, he could go to sleep if he liked, at
the fire. Joe went to sleep—how, I don't know. Then Dad
sat beside him, and for long intervals would stare silently

into the darkness. Sometimes a string of the vermin would hop past close to the fire, and another time a curlew would come near and screech its ghostly wail, but he never noticed them. Yet he seemed to be listening.

We mooched round from fire to fire, hour after hour, and when we wearied of heaving fire-sticks at the enemy we sat on our heels and cursed the wind, and the winter, and the night birds in turn. It was a lonely, wretched occupation.

Now and again Dad would leave his fire to ask us if we could hear a noise. We couldn't, except that of wallabies and mopokes. Then he would go back and listen again. He was restless and, somehow, his heart wasn't in the wallabies at all. Dave couldn't make him out.

The night wore on. By and by there was a sharp rattle of wires, then a rustling noise, and Sal appeared in the glare of the fire. "Dad!" she said. That was all. Without a word, Dad bounced up and went back to the house with her.

"Something's up!" Dave said, and, half anxious, half afraid, we gazed into the fire and thought and thought. Then we stared, nervously, into the night, and listened for Dad's return, but heard only the wind and the mopoke.

At dawn he appeared again, with a broad smile on his face, and told us that mother had got another baby—a fine little chap. *Then* we knew why Mrs Brown had been staying at our place.

Chapter VI

GOOD OLD BESS

SUPPER was over at Shingle Hut, and we were all seated round the fire—all except Joe. He was mousing. He stood on the sofa with one ear to the wall in a listening attitude, and brandished a table-fork. There were mice, mobs of them, between the slabs and the paper (layers of newspapers that had been pasted one on the other for years until they were an inch thick); and whenever Joe located a mouse he drove the fork into the wall and pinned it—or reckoned he did.

Dad sat pensively at one corner of the fireplace, Dave at the other, with his elbows on his knees and his chin resting in his palms.

"Think you could ride a race, Dave?" asked Dad.

"Yairs," answered Dave, without taking his eyes off the fire, or his chin from his palms. "Could, I suppose, if I'd a pair o' lighter boots 'n these."

Again they reflected.

Joe triumphantly held up the mutilated form of a murdered mouse and invited the household to look. No one heeded him.

"Would your Mother's go on you?"

"Might." And Dave spat into the fire.

"Anyway," Dad went on, "we must have a go at this handicap with the old mare. It's worth trying for, and, believe me, now, she'll surprise a few of their flash hacks, will Bess."

"Yairs, she can go all right." And Dave spat again into the fire.

"Go! I've never known anything to keep up with her. Why, bless my soul, seventeen years ago, when old Redwood owned her, there wasn't a horse in the district could come within cooee of her. All she wants is a few feeds of corn and a gallop or two, and mark my words she'll show some of them the way."

Some horse races were being promoted by the shanty-keeper at the Overhaul, seven miles from our selection. They were the first of the kind held in the district, and the stake for the principal event was five pounds. It wasn't because Dad was a racing man or subject in any way to turf hallucinations that he thought of preparing Bess for the meeting. We sadly needed those five pounds, and, as Dad put it, if the mare could only win, it would be an easier and much quicker way of making a bit of money than waiting for a crop to grow.

Bess was hobbled and put into a two-acre paddock near the house. We put her there because of her wisdom. She was a chestnut, full of villainy, an absolutely incorrigible old rogue. If at any time she was wanted when in the grass-paddock, it required the lot of us, from Dad down, to yard her, as well as our dogs and every other dog in the neighbourhood. Not that she had any brumby element in her—she would have been easier to yard if she had—but she would drive steadily enough, alone or with other horses, until she saw the yard, when she would turn and deliberately walk away. If we walked to head her she beat us by half a length; if we ran she ran, and stopped when we stopped. That was the aggravating part of her. When it was only to go to the store or the post office that we wanted her, we could have walked there and back a dozen times before we could run her down; but, somehow, we generally preferred to work hard catching her rather than walk.

When we had spent half the day hunting for the curry-comb, which we didn't find, Dad began to rub Bess down with a corn-cob—a shelled one—and trim her up a bit. He pulled her tail and cut the hair off her heels with a knife; then he gave her some corn to eat, and told Joe he was to have a bundle of thistles cut for her every night. Now and again, while grooming her, Dad would step back a few paces and look upon her with pride.

"There's great breeding in the old mare," he would say, "great breeding. Look at the shoulder on her, and the loin she has! And where did ever you see a horse with the same nostril? Believe me, she'll surprise a few of them!"

We began to regard Bess with profound respect; hitherto

29

we had been accustomed to pelt her with potatoes and blue-metal.

The only thing likely to prejudice her chance in the race, Dad reckoned, was a small sore on her back about the size of a foal's hoof. She had had that sore for upwards of ten years to our knowledge, but Dad hoped to have it cured before the race came off with a never-failing remedy he had discovered—burnt leather and fat.

Every day, along with Dad, we would stand on the fence near the house to watch Dave gallop Bess from the bottom of the lane to the barn—about a mile. We could always see him start, but immediately after he would disappear down a big gully, and we would see nothing more of the gallop till he came to within a hundred yards of us. And wouldn't Bess bend to it once she got up the hill, and fly past with Dave in the stirrups watching her shadow—when there was one! She was a little too fine to throw a shadow always. And when Dave and Bess had got back and Joe had led her round the yard a few times, Dad would rub the corn-cob over her again and apply more burnt leather and fat to her back.

On the morning preceding the race Dad decided to send Bess over three miles to improve her wind. Dave took her to the crossing at the creek—supposed to be three miles from Shingle Hut, but it might have been four or it might have been five, and there was a stony ridge on the way.

We mounted the fence and waited. Tommy Wilkie came along riding a plough-horse. He waited too.

"Ought to be coming now," Dad observed, and Wilkie got excited. He said he would go and wait in the gully and race Dave home. "Race him home!" Dad chuckled, as Tommy cantered off. "He'll never see the way Bess goes." Then we all laughed.

Just as someone cried "Here he is!" Dave turned the corner into the lane, and Joe fell off the fence and pulled

Dad with him. Dad damned him and scrambled up again as fast as he could. After a while Tommy Wilkie hove in sight amid a cloud of dust. Then came Dave at scarcely faster than a trot, and flogging all he knew with a piece of greenhide plough rein. Bess was all out and floundering. There was about two hundred yards yet to cover. Dave kept at her—*thud, thud!* Slower and slower she came. "Damn the fellow!" Dad said. "What's he beating her for? Stop it, you fool!" he shouted. But Dave sat down on her for the final effort and applied the hide faster and faster. Dad crunched his teeth. Once—twice—three times Bess changed her stride, then struck a branch root of a tree that projected a few inches above ground, and over she went—*crash!* Dave fell on his head and lay spread out, motionless. We picked him up and carried him inside, and when Mother saw blood on him she fainted straight off without waiting to know if it were his own or not. Both looked as good as dead, but Dad with a bucket of water, soon brought them round again.

It was scarcely dawn when we began preparing for a start to the races. Dave, after spending fully an hour trying in vain to pull on Mother's elastic-sided boots, decided to ride in his own heavy bluchers. We went with Dad in the dray. Mother wouldn't go. She said she didn't want to see her son get killed, and warned Dad that if anything happened the blame would for ever be on his head.

We arrived at the Overhaul in good time. Dad took the horse out of the dray and tied him to a tree. Dave led Bess about, and we stood and watched the shanty-keeper unpacking ginger-beer. Joe asked Dad for sixpence to buy some, but Dad hadn't any small change. We remained in front of the booth through most of the day, and ran after any corks that popped out and handed them in again to the shanty-keeper. He didn't offer us anything—not a thing.

"Saddle up for the Overhaul Handicap!" was at last sung

out, and Dad, saddle on arm, advanced to where Dave was walking Bess about. They saddled up and Dave mounted, looking as pale as death.

"I don't like ridin' in these boots a bit," he said with a quiver in his voice.

"What's up with 'em?" Dad asked.

"They're too big altogether."

"Well, take 'em off then!"

Dave jumped down and pulled them off, leaving his socks on.

More than a dozen horses went out, and when the starter said "Off!" didn't they go! Our eyes at once followed Bess. Dave was at her right from the jump—the very opposite to what Dad had told him. In the first furlong she put fully twenty yards of daylight between herself and the field—she came after the field. At the back of the course you could see the whole of Kyle's selection and two of Jerry Keefe's haystacks between her and the others. We didn't follow her any further.

After the race was won and they had cheered the winner, Dad wasn't to be found anywhere.

Dave sat on the grass quite exhausted. "Ain't y' goin' to pull the saddle off?" Joe asked.

"No," he said. "I *ain't*. You don't want everyone to see her back, do you?"

Joe wished he had sixpence.

About an hour afterwards Dad came staggering along arm-in-arm with another man, an old fencing· mate of his, so he made out.

"Thur y' are," he said, taking off his hat and striking Bess on the rump with it. "Besh-bred mare in the worl'."

The fencing mate looked at her, but didn't say anything. He couldn't.

"Eh?" Dad went on. "Say sh' ain't? L'ere—'ever y' name

is—betcher pound sh' is."

Then a jeering and laughing crowd gathered round, and Dave wished he hadn't come to the races.

"She ain't well," said a tall man to Dad. "Short in her gallops." Then a short, bulky individual without whiskers shoved his face up into Dad's and asked him if Bess was a mare or a cow. Dad became excited, and only that old Anderson came forward and took him away there would certainly have been a row.

Anderson put him in the dray and drove it home to Shingle Hut.

Dad reckons now that there is nothing in horse racing, and declares it a fraud. He says, further, that an honest man, by training and racing a horse, is only helping to feed and fatten the rogues and vagabonds that live on the sport.

Chapter VII

CRANKY JACK

IT was early in the day. Traveller after traveller was
trudging by Shingle Hut. One who carried no swag
halted at the rails and came in. He asked Dad for a job.
"I dunno," Dad answered. "What wages would you want?"
The man said he wouldn't want any. Dad engaged him at
once.

And *such* a man! Tall, bony, heavy-jawed, shaven with a reaping-hook, apparently. He had a thick crop of black hair, shaggy, unkempt, and full of grease, grass, and fragments of dry gum-leaves. On his head were two old felt hats, one sewn inside the other. On his back a shirt made from a piece of blue blanket, with white cotton stitches striding up and down it like lines of fencing. His trousers were gloom itself; they were a problem, and bore reliable evidence of his industry. No ordinary person would consider himself out of work while in them. And the new-comer was no ordinary person. He seemed to have all the woe of the world upon him. He was as sad and weird-looking as a widow out in the wet.

In the yard was a large heap of firewood—remarkable truth!—which Dad told him to chop up. He began. And how he worked! The axe rang again—particularly when it left the handle—and pieces of wood scattered everywhere. Dad watched him chopping for a while, then went with Dave to pull corn.

For hours the man chopped away without once looking at the sun. Mother came out. Joy! She had never seen so much wood cut before. She was delighted. She made a cup of tea and took it to the man, and apologized for having no sugar to put in it. He paid no attention to her; he worked harder. Mother waited, holding the tea in her hand. A lump of wood nearly as big as a shingle flew up and shaved her left ear. She put the tea on the ground and went in search of eggs for dinner. (We were out of meat—the kangaroo-dog was lame. He had got ripped the last time we killed.)

The tea remained on the ground. Chips fell into it. The dog saw it. He limped towards it eagerly, and dipped the point of his nose in it. It burnt him. An aged rooster strutted along and looked sideways at it. *He* distrusted it and went away. It attracted the pig, a sow with nine young ones. She waddled up, and poked the cup over with her nose; then she sat down on it, while the family joyously gathered round the saucer. Still the man chopped on.

Mother returned—without any eggs. She rescued the crockery from the pigs and turned curiously to the man. She said, "Why, you've let them take the tea!" No answer. She wondered.

Suddenly, and for the fiftieth time, the axe flew off. The man held the handle and stared at the woodheap. Mother watched him. He removed his hats, and looked inside them. He remained looking inside them.

Mother watched him more closely. His lips moved. He said, "*Listen to them! They're coming! I knew they'd follow!*"

"Who?" asked Mother, trembling slightly.

"*They're in the wood!*" he went on. "Ha, ha! I've got them. They'll never get out, *never get out!*"

Mother fled, screaming. She ran inside and called the children. Sal assisted her. They trooped in like wallabies, all but Joe. He was away earning money. He was getting a shilling a week from Maloney for chasing cockatoos from the corn.

They closed and barricaded the doors, and Sal took down the gun, which Mother made her hide beneath the bed. They sat listening, anxiously and intently. The wind began to rise. A lump of soot fell from the chimney into the fireplace, where there was no fire. Mother shuddered. Some more fell. Mother jumped to her feet. So did Sal. They looked at each other in dismay. The children began to cry. The chain for hanging the kettle on started swinging to and fro. Mother's knees gave way. The chain continued swinging. A pair of bare legs came down into the fireplace. They were curled round the chain. Mother collapsed. Sal screamed, and ran to the door, but couldn't open it. The legs left the chain and dangled in the air. Sal called, "Murder!"

Her cry was answered. It was Joe, who had been over at Maloney's making his fortune. He came to the rescue. He dropped out of the chimney and shook himself. Sal stared at him. He was calm and covered from head to foot with soot and dirt. He looked round and said, "Thought yuz could keep me out, didn'y'?" Sal could only look at him. "I saw yuz all run in," he was saying, when Sal thought of Mother, and sprang to her. Sal shook her, and slapped her, and threw water on her till she sat up and stared about. Then Joe stared.

Dad came in for dinner, which, of course, wasn't ready. Mother began to cry, and asked him what he meant by keeping a madman on the place, and told him she *knew* he wanted to have them all murdered. Dad didn't understand. Sal explained. Then he went out and said to the man, "Clear!"

The man simply said, "No."

"Go on, now!" Dad said, pointing to the rails. The man smiled at the woodheap as he worked. Dad waited. "Aren't y' going?" he repeated.

"Leave me alone when I'm chopping wood for the missus," the man answered, then smiled and muttered to himself. Dad left him alone and went inside wondering.

Next day Mother and Dad were talking at the barn. Mother, bare-headed, was holding some eggs in her apron. Dad was leaning on a hoe.

"I *am* afraid of him," Mother said. "It's not right you should keep him about the place. No one's safe with such a man. Some day he'll take it in his head to kill us all, and then—"

"Tut, tut, woman. Poor old Jack! He's harmless as a baby."

"All right," sullenly, "you'll see!"

E

Dad laughed and went away with the hoe on his shoulder to cut burr.

Middle of summer. Dad and Dave in the paddock mowing lucerne. Jack sinking post-holes for a milking-yard close to the house. Joe at intervals stealing behind him to prick him with straws through a rent in the rear of his patched moleskins. Little Bill, in readiness to run, standing off, enjoying the sport.

Inside the house sat Mother and Sal, sewing and talking of Maloney's new baby.

"Dear me," said Mother, "it's the tiniest mite of a thing I ever saw. Why, bless me, any one of y' at its age would have made three of—"

"*Mind*, Mother!" Sal shrieked, jumping up on the sofa. Mother screamed and mounted the table. Both gasped for breath, and leaning cautiously over peeped down at a big black snake which had glided in at the front door. Then, pale and scared-looking, they stared across at each other.

The snake crawled over to the safe and drank up some milk which had been spilt on the floor. Mother saw its full length and groaned. The snake wriggled to the leg of the table.

"Look out!" cried Sal, gathering up her skirts and dancing about on the sofa.

Mother squealed hysterically.

Joe appeared. He laughed.

"You wretch!" Mother yelled. "Run, *run*, and fetch your father!"

Joe went and brought Jack.

"Oh-h, my God!" Mother moaned, as Jack stood at the door staring strangely at her. "Kill it! Why don't he *kill* it?"

Jack didn't move, but talked to himself. Mother shuddered.

The reptile crawled to the bedroom door. Then for the first time the man's eyes rested upon it. It glided into the bedroom, and Mother and Sal ran off for Dad.

Jack fixed his eyes on the snake and continued muttering to himself. Several times it made an attempt to mount the dressing-table. Finally it succeeded. Suddenly Jack's demeanour changed. He threw off his ragged hat and talked wildly. A fearful expression filled his ugly features. His voice altered.

"You're the Devil!" he said. "The *Devil*! The DEVIL! The missus brought you—ah-h-h!"

The snake's head passed behind the looking-glass. Jack drew nearer, clenching his fists and gesticulating. As he did he came full before the looking-glass and saw, perhaps for the first time in his life, his own image. An unearthly howl came from him. "*Me father!*" he shouted, and bolted from the house.

Dad came in with the long-handled shovel, swung it about the room, and smashed pieces off the cradle, and tore the bed-curtains down, and made a great noise altogether. Finally, he killed the snake and put it on the fire, and Joe and the cat watched it wriggle on the hot coals.

Meanwhile, Jack, bare-headed, rushed across the yard. He ran over Little Bill, and tumbled through the wire fence on to the broad of his back. He roared like a wild beast, clutched at space, spat, and kicked his heels in the air.

"Let me up! *Ah-h-h!* Let go me throat!" he hissed.

The dog ran over and barked at him. He found his feet again, and, making off, ran through the wheat, glancing back over his shoulder as he tore along. He crossed into the grass-paddock, and running to a big tree dodged round and round it. Then from tree to tree he went, and that evening at sundown, when Joe was bringing the cows home, Jack was still flying from his "father".

After supper.

"I wonder now what the old fool saw in that snake to send

him off his head like that?" Dad said, gazing wonderingly into the fire. "He sees plenty of them, goodness knows."

"That wasn't it. It wasn't the snake at all," Mother said. "There was madness in the man's eyes all the while. I saw it the moment he came to the door." She appealed to Sal.

"Nonsense!" said Dad. "*Nonsense!*" And he tried to laugh.

"Oh, of course it's *nonsense*," Mother went on. "Everything I say is nonsense. It won't be nonsense when you come home some day and find us all on the floor with our throats cut."

"Pshaw!" Dad answered. "What's the use of talking like that?" Then to Dave, "Go out and see if he's in the barn."

Dave fidgeted. He didn't like the idea. Joe giggled.

"Surely you're not *frightened*?" Dad shouted.

Dave coloured up.

"No—don't think so," he said, and, after a pause, "*You* go and see."

It was Dad's turn to feel uneasy. He pretended to straighten the fire and coughed several times. "Perhaps it's just as well," he said, "to let him be tonight."

Of course, Dad wasn't afraid. He *said* he wasn't. But he drove the pegs in the doors and windows before going to bed that night.

Next morning Dad said to Dave and Joe, "Come 'long, and we'll see where he's got to."

In a gully at the back of the grass-paddock they found him. He was ploughing—sitting astride the highest limb of a fallen tree—and, in a hoarse voice and strange, was calling out, "Gee, Captain! Come here, Tidy! *Wa-ay!*"

"Blowed if I know," Dad muttered, coming to a standstill. "Wonder if he *is* clean mad?"

Dave was speechless, and Joe began to tremble.

They listened. And as the man's voice rang out in the

quiet gully and the echoes rumbled round the ridge and the affrighted birds flew up the place felt eerie somehow.

"It's no use bein' afraid of him," Dad went on. "We must go and bounce him, that's all." But there was a tremor in Dad's voice which Dave didn't like.

"See if he knows us, anyway." And Dad shouted "*Hey-y!*"

Jack looked up and immediately scrambled from the limb. That was enough for Dave. He turned and made tracks. So did Dad and Joe. They ran. No one could have run harder. Terror overcame Joe. He squealed and grabbed hold of Dad's shirt, which was ballooning in the wind.

"Let go!" Dad gasped. "*Damn* y', let me *go!*"—trying to shake him off. But Joe had great faith in his parent, and clung to him closely.

When they had covered a hundred yards or so, Dave glanced back, and, seeing that Jack wasn't pursuing them, stopped and chuckled at the others.

"Eh?" Dad said, completely winded. "Eh?" Then to Dave, when he got some breath, "Well, you *are* an ass of a fellow—*puff*. What the devil did *you* run f'?"

"What did *I* run f'? What did *you* run f'?"

"Bah!" And Dad boldly led the way back.

"Now look here"—turning fiercely upon Joe—"don't you come catching hold of me again, or if y' *do* I'll knock y'r damned head off! Clear home altogether, and get under the bed if y're as frightened as *that*."

Joe slunk behind.

But when Dad *did* approach Jack, which wasn't until he had talked a great deal to him across a big log, the latter didn't show any desire to take life, but allowed himself to be escorted home and locked in the barn quietly enough.

Dad kept Jack confined in the barn several days, and if anyone approached the door or the cracks he would ask, "Is me father there yet?"

41

"Your father's dead and buried long ago, man," Dad used to tell him.

"Yes," he would say, "but he's alive again. The missus keeps him in there"—indicating the house.

And sometimes when Dad was not about Joe would put his mouth to a crack and say, "Here's y'r *father*, Jack!"

Then, like a caged beast, the man would howl and tramp up and down, his eyes starting out of his head, while Joe would bolt inside and say to Mother, "Jack's getting out", and nearly send her to her grave.

But one day Jack *did* get out, and while Mother and Sal were ironing came to the door with the axe on his shoulder.

They dropped the irons and shrank into a corner and cowered piteously—too scared even to cry out.

He took no notice of them, but, moving stealthily on tip-toes, approached the bedroom door and peeped in. He paused just a moment to grip the axe with both hands. Then with a howl and a bound he entered the room and shattered the looking-glass into fragments.

He bent down and looked closely at the pieces.

"He's dead now," he said calmly, and walked out. Then he went to work at the post-holes again, just as though nothing had happened.

The man stayed on at Shingle Hut. He was the best horse Dad ever had. He slaved from daylight till dark, kept no Sunday, knew no companion, lived chiefly on meat and machine oil, domiciled in the barn, and never asked for a rise in his wages. His name we never knew. We called him "Jack". The neighbours called him "*Cranky* Jack".

Chapter VIII

A KANGAROO HUNT FROM SHINGLE HUT

W<small>E</small> always looked forward to Sundays. It was our day of sport. Once, I remember, we thought it would never come. We longed restlessly for it, and the more we longed the more it seemed to linger.

A meeting of selectors had been held, war declared against the marsupial, and a hunt on a grand scale arranged for this particular Sabbath. Of course, those in the neighbourhood hunted the kangaroo every Sunday, but "on their own", and always on foot, which had its fatigues. This was to be a raid *en masse* and on horseback. The whole countryside was to assemble at Shingle Hut and proceed thence. It assembled—and what a collection! Such a crowd! Such gear! Such a tame lot of horses! And *such* a motley swarm of lean, lank, lame kangaroo-dogs!

We were not ready. The crowd sat on their horses and waited at the slip-rails. Dogs trooped into the yard by the dozen. One pounced on a fowl, another lamed the pig, a trio put the cat up a peach-tree, one with a thirst mounted the water-cask and looked down it, while the bulk of the brutes trotted inside and disputed with Mother who should open the safe.

Dad loosed our three, and pleased they were to feel themselves free. They had been chained up all the week, with scarcely anything to eat. Dad didn't believe in too much feeding. He had had wide experience in dogs and coursing at Home on his grandfather's large estates, and always found

43

them fleetest when empty. *Ours* ought to have been as fleet as locomotives.

Dave, showing a neat seat, rode out of the yard on Bess, fresh and fat and fit to run for a kingdom. They waited for Dad. He was standing beside *his* mount—Farmer, the plough-horse, who was arrayed in winkers with greenhide reins, and an old saddle with only one flap. He was holding an earnest argument with Joe. Still the crowd waited. Still Dad and Joe argued the point. There was a murmur and a movement and much merriment. Dad was coming; so was Joe—perched behind him, double bank, rapidly wiping the tears from his eyes with his knuckles.

Hooray! They were off. Paddy Maloney and Dave took the lead, heading for kangaroo country along the foot of Dead Man's Mountain and through Smith's paddock, where there was a low wire fence to negotiate. Paddy spread his coat over it and jumped his mare across. He was a horseman, was Pat. The others twisted a stick in the wires, and proceeded carefully to lead their horses over. When it came to Farmer's turn he hesitated. Dad coaxed him. Slowly he put one leg across, as if feeling his way, and paused again. Joe was on his back behind the saddle. Dad tugged hard at the winkers. Farmer was inclined to withdraw his leg. Dad was determined not to let him. Farmer's heel got caught against the wire, and he began to pull back and grunt. So did Dad. Both pulled hard. Anderson and old Brown ran to Dad's assistance. The trio planted their heels in the ground and leant back. Joe became afraid. He clutched at the saddle and cried, "Let me off!" "Stick to him!" said Paddy Maloney, hopping over the fence. "Stick to him!" He kicked Farmer what he afterwards called "a sollicker on the tail". Again he kicked him. Still Farmer strained and hung back. Once more he let him have it. Then, off flew the winkers, and over went Dad and Anderson and old Brown, and down rolled

44

A Kangaroo Hunt from Shingle Hut

Joe and Farmer on the other side of the fence. The others leant against their horses and laughed the laugh of their lives. "Worse 'n a lot of damned jackasses," Dad was heard to say. They caught Farmer and led him to the fence again. He jumped it, and rose feet higher than he had any need to, and had not old Brown dodged him just when he did he would be a dead man now.

A little further on the huntsmen sighted a mob of kangaroos. Joy and excitement. A mob—it was a swarm! Away they hopped. Off scrambled the dogs, and off flew Paddy Maloney and Dave. The rest followed anyhow, and at varying speeds.

That all those dogs should have selected and followed the same kangaroo was sad and humiliating. And such a waif of a thing, too! Still, they stuck to it. For more than a mile, down a slope, the weedy marsupial outpaced them, but when it came to the hill the daylight between rapidly began to lessen. A few seconds more and all would have been over, but a straggling, stupid old ewe, belonging to an unneighbourly squatter, darted up from the shade of a tree right in the way of Maloney's Brindle, who was leading. Brindle always preferred mutton to marsupial, so he let the latter slide and secured the ewe. The death scene was most imposing. The ground around was strewn with small tufts of white wool. There was a complete circle of eager, wriggling dogs, all jammed together, heads down, and tails elevated. Not a scrap of the ewe was visible. Paddy Maloney jumped down and proceeded to batter the brutes vigorously with a waddy. As the others arrived they joined him. The dogs were hungry, and fought for every inch of the sheep. Those not laid out were pulled away, and when old Brown had dragged the last one off by the hind-legs, all that was left of that ewe was four feet and some skin.

Dad shook his head and looked grave; so did Anderson.

After a short rest they decided to divide into parties and work the ridges. A start was made. Dad's contingent, consisting of himself and Joe, Paddy Maloney, Anderson, old Brown, and several others, started a mob. This time the dogs separated and scampered off in all directions. In quick time Brown's black slut bailed up an "old man" full of fight. Nothing was more desirable. He was a monster, a king kangaroo, and as he raised himself to his full height on his toes and tail he looked formidable—a grand and majestic demon of the bush. The slut made no attempt to tackle him; she stood off with her tongue out. Several small dogs belonging to Anderson barked energetically at him, even venturing occasionally to run behind and bite his tail. But, further than grabbing them in his arms and embracing them, he took no notice. There he towered, his head back and chest well out, awaiting the horsemen. They came, shouting and hooraying. He faced them defiantly. Anderson, aglow with excitement, dismounted and aimed a lump of rock at his head, which laid out one of the little dogs. They pelted him with sticks and stones till their arms were tired, but they might just as well have pelted a dead cow. Paddy Maloney took out his stirrup. "Look out!" he cried. They looked out. Then, galloping up, he swung the iron at the marsupial and nearly knocked his horse's eye out.

Dad was disgusted. He and Joe approached the enemy on Farmer. Dad carried a short stick. The old man looked him straight in the face. Dad poked the stick at him. He promptly grabbed hold of it, and a piece of Dad's hand as well. Farmer had not been in many battles—no Defence Force man ever owned him. He threw up his head and snorted, and commenced a retreat. The kangaroo followed him up and seized Dad by the shirt. Joe evinced signs of timidity. He lost faith in Dad, and, half jumping, half falling, he landed on the ground, and set out speedily for a tree. Dad lost the stick, and in attempting to brain the brute with his fist he overbalanced and fell out of the saddle. He struggled to his feet and clutched his antagonist affectionately by both paws—standing well away. Backwards and forwards and round and round they moved. "Use your knife!" Anderson called out, getting farther away himself. But Dad dared not relax his grip. Paddy Maloney ran behind the brute several times to lay him out with a waddy, but each time he turned and fled before striking the blow. Dad thought to force matters, and began kicking his assailant vigorously in the stomach. Such dull, heavy thuds! The kangaroo retaliated, putting Dad on the defensive. Dad displayed remarkable suppleness about the hips. At last the brute fixed his deadly toe in Dad's belt.

It was an anxious moment, but the belt broke, and Dad breathed freely again. He was acting entirely on the defensive, but an awful consciousness of impending misfortune assailed him. His belt was gone, and his trousers began to slip—slip—slip! He called wildly to the others for God's sake to do something. They helped with advice. He yelled "Curs!" and "Cowards!" back at them. Still, as he danced around with his strange and ungainly partner, his trousers kept slipping—slipping. For the fiftieth time and more he glanced eagerly over his shoulder for some haven of safety. None was near. And then—oh, horror!—down they slid calmly and noiselessly. Poor Dad! He was at a disadvantage; his leg work was hampered; he was hobbled. Could he only get free of them altogether! But he couldn't—his feet were large. He took a lesson from the foe and jumped—jumped this way and that way, and round about, while large drops of sweat rolled off him. The small dogs displayed renewed and ridiculous ferocity, often mistaking Dad for the marsupial. At last Dad became exhausted—there was no spring left in him. Once he nearly went down. Twice he tripped.

He staggered again—down he was going—down—down—and down he fell! But at the same moment, and, as though they had dropped from the clouds, Brindle and five or six other dogs pounced on the old man. The rest may be imagined.

Dad lay on the ground to recover his wind, and when he mounted Farmer again and silently turned for home, Paddy Maloney was triumphantly seated on the carcass of the fallen enemy, exultingly explaining how he missed the brute's head with the stirrup-iron, and claiming the tail.

Chapter IX

DAVE'S SNAKE-BITE

ONE hot day, as we were finishing dinner, a sheriff's bailiff rode up to the door. Norah saw him first. She was dressed up ready to go over to Mrs Anderson's to tea. Sometimes young Harrison had tea at Anderson's—Thursdays, usually. This was Thursday, and Norah was starting early, because it was "a good step of a way". She reported the visitor. Dad left the table, munching some bread, and went out to him. Mother looked out of the door, Sal went to the window, Little Bill and Tom peeped through a crack, Dave remained at his dinner, and Joe knavishly seized the opportunity of exploring the table for leavings, finally seating himself in Dad's place, and commencing where Dad had left off.

"Jury summons," said the meek bailiff, extracting a paper from his breast-pocket, and reading, " 'Murtagh Joseph Rudd, selector, Shingle Hut' . . . Correct?"

Dad nodded assent.

"Got any water?"

There wasn't a drop in the cask, so Dad came in and asked Mother if there was any tea left. She pulled a long, solemn, Sunday-school face, and looked at Joe, who was holding the teapot upsidedown shaking the tea-leaves into his cup.

"Tea, Dad?" he asked chuckling. "By golly!"

Dad didn't think it worth while going out to the bailiff again. He sent Joe.

"Not any at all?"

"Nothink," said Joe.

"H'm! *Nulla bona*, eh?" And the Law smiled at its own joke and went off thirsty.

Thus it was that Dad came to be away one day when his great presence of mind and ability as a bush doctor were most required at Shingle Hut.

Dave took Dad's place at the plough. One of the horses, a colt that Dad bought with the money he got for helping with Anderson's crop, had only just been broken. He was bad at starting. When touched with the rein he would stand and wait until the old furrow-horse put in a few steps, then plunge to get ahead of him. If a chain or a swingle-tree or something else didn't break, and Dave kept the plough in, he ripped and tore along in style, bearing in and bearing out, and knocking the old horse about till that much-enduring animal became as cranky as himself, and the pace terrible. Down would go the plough-handles, and, with one tremendous pull on the reins, Dave would haul them back on their rumps. Then he would rush up and kick the colt on the root of the tail, and if that didn't make him put his leg over the chains and kick till he ran a hook into his heel and lamed himself, or broke something, it caused him to rear up and fall back on the plough and snort and strain and struggle till there was not a stitch left on him but the winkers.

Now, if Dave was noted for one thing more than another

it was for his silence. He scarcely ever took the trouble to speak. He hated to be asked a question, and mostly answered by nodding his head. Yet, though he never seemed to practise, he could, when his blood was fairly up, swear with distinction and effect. On this occasion he swore through the whole afternoon without repeating himself.

Towards evening Joe took the reins and began to drive. He hadn't gone once round when, just as the horses approached a big dead tree that had been left standing in the cultivation, he planted his left foot heavily upon a Bathurst burr that had been cut and left lying. It clung to him. He hopped along on one leg, trying to kick it off. Still it clung to him. He fell down. The horses and the tree got mixed up, and everything was confusion.

Dave abused Joe remorselessly. "Go on!" he howled, waving in the air a fistful of grass and weeds which he had pulled from the nose of the plough. "Clear out of this altogether. You're only a damn nuisance."

Joe's eyes rested on the fistful of grass. They lit up suddenly.

"L-l-look out, Dave," he stuttered, "y'-y' got a s-s-snake."

Dave dropped the grass promptly. A death adder crawled out of it. Joe killed it. Dave looked closely at his hand, which was all scratches and scars. He looked at it again; then he sat on the beam of the plough, pale and miserable-looking.

"D-d-did it bite y', Dave?" No answer.

Joe saw a chance to distinguish himself, and took it. He ran home, glad to be the bearer of the news, and said to Mother, "Dave's got bit by a adder—a sudden-death adder—right on top o' the finger."

How Mother screamed! "My God! What ever shall we do? Run quick," she said, "and bring Mr Maloney. Dear, oh dear, oh dear!"

Joe had not calculated on this injunction. He dropped his

head and said sullenly, "What, walk all the way over there?"

Before he could say another word a tin dish left a dint on the back of his skull that will accompany him to his grave if he lives to be a thousand.

"You wretch, you! Why don't you run when I tell you?" Joe sprang in the air like a shot wallaby.

"I'll not go *at all* now—y' see!" he answered, starting to cry. Then Sal put on her hat and ran for Maloney.

Meanwhile Dave took the horses out, walked inside, and threw himself on the sofa without uttering a word. He felt ill.

Mother was in a paroxysm of fright. She threw her arms about frantically and cried for someone to come. At last she sat down and tried to think what she could do. She thought of the very thing, and ran for the carving knife, which she handed to Dave with shut eyes. He motioned her with a disdainful movement of the elbow to take it away.

Would Maloney never come? He *was* coming, hat in hand, and running for dear life across the potato paddock. Behind him was his man. Behind this man, Sal, out of breath. Behind her, Mrs Maloney and the children.

"Phwat's the thrubble?" cried Maloney. "Bit be a dif adher? Oh, be the tares of war!" Then he asked Dave numerous questions as to how it happened, which Joe answered with promptitude and pride. Dave simply shrugged his shoulders and turned his face to the wall. Nothing was to be got out of *him*.

Maloney held a short consultation with himself. Then, "Hould up y' hand!" he said, bending over Dave with a knife. Dave thrust out his arm violently, knocked the instrument to the other side of the room, and kicked wickedly.

"The pison's wurrkin'," whispered Maloney quite loud.

"Oh, my gracious!" groaned Mother.

"The poor crathur," said Mrs Maloney.

52

"Phwat finger's bit?" asked Maloney. Joe thought it was the littlest one of the lot.

He approached the sofa again, knife in hand.

"Show me y' finger," he said to Dave.

For the first time Dave spoke. He said, "*Damm* y'. What the devil do y' want? Clear out and lea' me 'lone."

Maloney hesitated. There was a long silence. Dave commenced breathing heavily.

"It's makin' 'im slape," whispered Maloney, glancing over his shoulder at the women.

"Don't let him! Don't let him!" Mother wailed.

"Salvation to 's all!" muttered Mrs Maloney, piously crossing herself.

Maloney put away the knife and beckoned to his man, who was looking on from the door. They both took a firm hold of Dave and stood him upon his feet. He looked hard and contemptuously at Maloney for some seconds. Then with gravity and deliberation Dave said, "Now what 'n the *devil* are y' up t'? Are y' *mad*?"

"Walk 'im along, James—walk 'im along," was all Maloney had to say. And out into the yard they marched him. How Dave did struggle to get away!—swearing and cursing Maloney for a cranky Irishman till he foamed at the mouth, all of which the other put down to snake poison. Round and round the yard and up and down it they trotted him till long after dark, until there wasn't a struggle left in him.

They placed him on the sofa again, Maloney keeping him awake with a strap. How Dave ground his teeth and kicked and swore whenever he felt that strap! And they sat and watched him.

It was late in the night when Dad came from town. He staggered in with the neck of a bottle showing out of his pocket. In his hand was a piece of paper wrapped round the

F

end of some yards of sausage. The dog outside carried the other end.

"An' 'e ishn't dead?" Dad said, after hearing what had befallen Dave. "Don' b'leevsh id. Wuzhn't bit. Die 'fore shun'own ifsh desh adder bish 'm."

"Bit!" Dave said bitterly, turning round to the surprise of everyone. "I never said I was *bit*. No one said I was, only those snivelling idiots and that pumpkin-headed Irish pig there."

Maloney lowered his jaw and opened his eyes.

"Zhackly. Didn' I—*hic*—shayzo, 'Loney? Didn' I, eh, ol' wom'n?" Dad mumbled, and dropped his chin on his chest.

Maloney began to take another view of the matter. He put a leading question to Joe.

"He *muster* been bit," Joe answered, " 'cuz he had the d-death adder in his hand."

More silence.

"Mush die 'fore shun'own," Dad murmured.

Maloney was thinking hard. At last he spoke. "Bridgy!" he cried. "Where's the childer?" Mrs Maloney gathered them up.

Just then Dad seemed to be dreaming. He swayed about. His head hung lower, and he muttered, "Shen'l'm'n, yoush disharged with shanksh y' coun'ry."

The Maloneys left.

Dave is still alive and well, and silent as ever, and if any one question is more intolerable and irritating to him than another, it is to be asked if he remembers the time he was bitten by a death adder.

Chapter X

DAD AND THE DONOVANS

A SWELTERING summer's afternoon. A heat that curled and withered the very weeds. The corn-blades drooping, sulking still. Mother and Sal ironing, mopping their faces with a towel and telling each other how hot it was. The dog stretched across the doorway. A child's bonnet on the floor, the child out in the sun. Two horsemen approaching the slip-rails.

Dad had gone down the gully to Farmer, who had been sick for four days. The ploughing was at a standstill in consequence, for we had only two draught-horses. Dad erected a shelter over him, made of boughs, to keep the sun off. Two or three times a day he cut greenstuff for him—which the cows ate. He humped water to him, which he sullenly refused to drink, and did all in his power to persuade Farmer to get up and go on with the ploughing. I don't know if Dad knew anything of mesmerism, but he used to stand for long intervals dumbly staring the old horse full in the eyes till in a commanding voice he would bid him, "Get up!" But Farmer lacked the patriotism of the back-block poets. He was obdurate, and not once did he "awake", not to mention "arise".

This afternoon, as Dad approached his dumb patient, he suddenly put down the bucket of water which he was carrying and ran, shouting angrily. A flock of crows flew away from Farmer and cawed from a tree close by. Dad was excited, and when he saw that one of the animal's eyes was

55

gone and a stream of blood trickled over its nose he sat down and hid his face in his big rough hands.

"*Caw, caw!*" came from the tree.

Dad rose and looked up.

"*Curse* you!" he hissed. "You black wretches of hell!"

"*Caw, caw, caw!*"

He ran towards the tree as though he would hurl it to the ground, and away flew the crows.

Joe arrived.

"W-w-wuz they at him, Dad?"

Dad turned on him, trembling with rage.

"Oh, *you* son of the Devil!" he commenced. "*You* worthless pup, you! Look there! Do you see that?" He pointed to the horse. "Didn't I tell you to mind him? Didn't—"

"Yes," snivelled Joe, "but Anderson's dog had a k-k-k-angaroo bailed up."

"*Damn* you, be off out of this!" And Dad aimed a block of wood at Joe which struck him on the back as he made away. But nothing short of two broken legs would stop Joe, who the next instant had dashed among the corn like an emu into a scrub.

Dad returned to the house, foaming and vowing to take the gun and shoot Joe down like a wallaby. But when he saw two horses hanging up he hesitated and would have gone away again had Mother not called out that he was wanted. He went in reluctantly.

Red Donovan and his son, Mick, were there. Donovan was the publican, butcher, and horse-dealer at the Overhaul. He was reputed to be well in, though some said that if everybody had their own he wouldn't be worth much. He was a glib-tongued Irishman who knew everything—or fondly imagined he did—from the law to horse surgery. There was money to be made out of selections, he reckoned, if selectors only knew how to make it. The majority, he proclaimed, didn't know enough to get under a tree when it rained. As a dealer he was a hard nut, never giving more than a tenner for a twenty-pound beast, or selling a ten-pound one for less than twenty pounds. And few knew Donovan better than did Dad, or had been taken in by him oftener. But on this occasion Dad was in no easy or benevolent frame of mind.

He sat down, and they talked of crops and the weather and beat about the bush until Donovan said, "Have you any fat steers to sell?"

Dad hadn't. "But," he said, "I can sell you a horse."

"Which one?" asked Donovan, for he knew the horses as well as Dad did—perhaps better.

"The bay—Farmer."

"How much?"

"Seven pounds." Now, Farmer was worth fourteen pounds, if worth a shilling—that is, before he took sick—and Donovan knew it well.

"Seven," he repeated ponderingly. "Give you six."

Never before did Dad show himself such an expert in dissimulation. He shook his head knowingly, and inquired of Donovan if he would take the horse for nothing.

"Split the difference, then. Make it six ten."

Dad rose and looked out the window. "There he is now," he remarked sadly, "in the gully there."

"Well, what's it to be—six ten or nothing?" asked Donovan.

"All right, then," Dad replied demurely. "Take him!"

The money was paid there and then and receipts drawn up. Then, saying that Mick would come for the horse on the day following, and after offering a little gratuitous advice on seed wheat and pig-sticking, the Donovans left.

Mick came the next day, and Dad showed him Farmer, under the bushes. He wasn't dead, because when Joe sat on him he moved. "There he is," said Dad, grinning.

Mick remained seated on his horse, bewildered-looking, staring first at Farmer, then at Dad.

"Well?" Dad remarked, still grinning. Then Mick spoke feelingly.

"*You swindling old crawler!*" he said, and galloped away. It was well for him he got a good start.

For long after that we turned the horses and cows into the little paddock at night, and if ever the dog barked Dad would jump up and go out in his shirt.

We put them back into the paddock again, and the first night they were there two cows got out and went away, taking with them the chain that fastened the slip-rails. We never saw or heard of them again; but Dad treasured them in his heart. Often, when he was thoughtful, he would ponder over plans for getting even with the Donovans—we knew it was the Donovans. And Fate seemed to be of Dad's mind, for the Donovans got into "trouble", and were reported to be doing time. That pleased Dad, but the vengeance was a little vague. He would have liked a finger in the pie himself.

Four years passed. It was after supper, and we were all husking corn in the barn. Old Anderson and young Tom Anderson and Mrs Maloney were helping us. We were to assist them the following week. The barn was illuminated by fat-lamps, which made the spiders in the rafters uneasy and disturbed the slumbers of a few fowls that for months had insisted on roosting on the cross-beam.

Mrs Maloney was arguing with Anderson. She was claiming to have husked two cobs to his one, when the dogs started barking savagely. Dad crawled from beneath a heap of husks and went out. The night was dark. He bade the dogs lie down. They barked louder. "*Damn* you, lie down!" he roared. They shut up. Then a voice from the darkness said, "Is that you, Mr Rudd?"

Dad failed to recognize it, and went to the fence where the visitor was. He remained there talking for fully half an hour. Then he returned, and said it was young Donovan.

"*Donovan! Mick* Donovan?" exclaimed Anderson. And Mother and Mrs Maloney and Joe echoed "*Mick* Donovan?" They *were* surprised.

"He's none too welcome," said Anderson, thinking of his horses and cows. Mother agreed with him, while Mrs Maloney repeated over and over again that she was always under the impression that Mick Donovan was in jail along with his bad old father. Dad was uncommunicative. There was something on his mind. He waited till the company had gone, then consulted with Dave.

They were outside, in the dark, and leant on the dray. Dad said in a low voice, "He's come a hundred miles today, 'n' his horse is dead-beat, 'n' he wants one t' take him t' Back Creek t'morrow 'n' leave this one in his place. . . . What d'y' think?" Dave seemed to think a great deal, for he said nothing.

"Now," continued Dad, "it's my opinion the horse isn't his. It's one he's shook—an' I've an idea." Then he proceeded to instruct Dave in the idea. A while later he called Joe and drilled him in the idea.

That night young Donovan stayed at Shingle Hut. In the morning Dad was very affable. He asked Donovan to come and show him his horse, because he must see it before thinking of exchanging. They proceeded to the paddock together. The horse was standing under a tree, tired-looking. Dad stood and looked at Donovan for fully half a minute without speaking.

"Why, damn it!" he exclaimed at last. "That's *my own* horse. You don't mean. . . . S'help me! Old Bess's foal!"

Donovan told him he was making a mistake.

"Mistake be hanged!" replied Dad, walking round the animal. "Not much of a mistake about *him*!"

Just here Dave appeared, as was proper.

"Do you know this horse?" Dad asked him. "Yes, of course," he answered surprisedly, with his eyes wide open. "Bess's foal! Of course it is."

"There you are!" said Dad, grinning triumphantly.

Donovan seemed uneasy.

Joe in his turn appeared. Dad put the same question to him. Of course Joe knew Bess's foal, "the one that got stole."

There was a silence.

"Now," said Dad, looking very grave, "what have y' got t' say? Who'd y' get him off? Show's y'r receipt."

Donovan had nothing to say. He preferred to be silent.

"Then," Dad went on, "clear out of this as fast as you can go, an' think y'rself lucky."

He cleared, but on foot.

Dad gazed after him, and, as he left the paddock, said, "One too many f' y' that time, Mick Donovan!" Then to Dave, who was still looking at the horse, "He's a stolen one right enough, but he's a beauty, and we'll keep him; and if the owner ever comes for him, well—if he is the owner—he can have him, that's all."

We had the horse for eighteen months and more. One day Dad rode him to town. He was no sooner there than a man came up and claimed him. Dad objected. The man went off and brought a policeman. "Orright," Dad said, "*take* him." The policeman took him. He took Dad too. The lawyer got Dad off, but it cost us five bags of potatoes. Dad didn't grudge them, for he reckoned we'd had value. Besides he was even with the Donovans for the two cows.

Chapter XI

A SPLENDID YEAR FOR CORN

WE had just finished supper. Supper! Dry bread and
sugarless tea. Dad was tired out and was resting at
one end of the sofa. Joe was stretched at the other,
without a pillow, and his legs tangled up among Dad's. Bill
and Tom squatted in the ashes, while Mother tried to put
the fat-lamp into burning order by poking it with a table-
fork.

Dad was silent. He seemed sad, and lay for some time
gazing at the roof. He might have been watching the blaze
of the glorious moon or counting the stars through the
gaps in the shingles, but he wasn't. There was no such senti-
ment in Dad. He was thinking how his long years of toil and
worry had been rewarded again and again by disappoint-
ment, wondering if ever there would be a turn in his luck,

and how he was going to get enough out of the land that season to pay interest and keep Mother and us in bread and meat.

At last he spoke, or rather muttered disjointedly, "Plen-ty —to eat—in the safe." Then suddenly, in a strange and hollow voice, he shouted, "*They're dead—all of them! I starved them!*"

Mother *did* get a fright. She screamed. Then Dad jumped up, rubbing his eyes, and asked what was the matter. Nothing was the matter *then*. He had dozed and talked in his sleep, that was all, he hadn't starved anyone. Joe didn't jump up when Mother screamed—not altogether. He raised himself and reached for Dad's pillow, then lay down and snored serenely till bed-time.

Dad sat gloomily by the fire and meditated. Mother spoke pleadingly to him and asked him not to fret. He ran his fingers uneasily through his hair and spat in the ashes. "Don't fret? When there's not a bit to eat in the place, when there's no way of getting anything, and when—merciful God!—every year sees things worse than they were before."

"It's only fancy," Mother went on. "And you've been brooding and brooding till it seems far worse than it really is."

"It's no fancy, Ellen." Then, after a pause, "Was the thirty acres of wheat that didn't come up fancy? Is it only fancy that we've lost nearly every beast in the paddock? Was the drought itself a fancy? No—no." And he shook his head sadly and stared again into the fire.

Dad's inclination was to leave the selection, but Mother pleaded for another trial of it—just one more. She had wonderful faith in the selection, had Mother. She pleaded until the fire burnt low. Then Dad rose and said, "Well, we'll try it once more with corn, and if nothing comes of it, why then we *must* give it up."

Then he took the spade and raked the fire together and covered it with ashes—we always covered the fire over before going to bed so as to keep it alight. Some mornings, though, it would be out, when one of us would have to go across to Anderson's and borrow a fire-stick. Any of us but Joe—he was sent only once, and on that occasion he stayed at Anderson's for breakfast, and on his way back successfully burnt out two grass-paddocks belonging to a J.P.

So we began to prepare the soil for another crop of corn, and Dad started over the same old ground with the same old plough. How I remember that old, screwed and twisted plough! The land was very hard, and the horses out of condition. We wanted a furrow-horse. Smith had one—a good one. "Put him in the furrow," he said to Dad, "and you can't *pull* him out of it." Dad wished to have such a horse. Smith offered to exchange his for our roan saddle-mare—one that we had found running in the lane, and advertised as being in our paddock, and that no one had claimed. Dad exchanged.

He yoked the new horse to the plough, and it took to the furrow splendidly, but that was all. It didn't take to anything else. Dad gripped the handles. "Git up!" he said, and tapped Smith's horse with the rein. Smith's horse pranced and marked time well, but didn't tighten the chains. Dad touched him again. Then he stood on his fore-legs and threw about a hundredweight of mud that clung to his heels at Dad's head. That aggravated Dad, and he seized the plough-scraper, and, using both hands, calmly belted Smith's horse over the ribs for two minutes, by the sun. He tried him again. The horse threw himself down in the furrow. Dad took the scraper again, welted him on the rump, dug it into his back-bone, prodded him in the side, then threw it at him disgustedly. Then Dad sat down awhile and breathed heavily. He rose again and pulled Smith's horse by the head. He was pulling hard when Dave and Joe came up. Joe had a bow and arrow

63

in his hand, and said, "He's a good furrer-'orse, eh, Dad? Smith *said* you couldn't pull him out of it."

Shall I ever forget the look on Dad's face! He brandished the scraper and sprang wildly at Joe and yelled, "Damn y', you *whelp*! What do you want here?"

Joe left. The horse lay in the furrow. Blood was dropping from its mouth. Dave pointed it out, and Dad opened the brute's jaws and examined them. No teeth were there. He looked on the ground round about—none there either. He looked at the horse's mouth again, then hit him viciously with his clenched fist and said, "The old ——, he never *did* have any!" At length he unharnessed the brute as it lay, pulled the winkers off, hurled them at its head, kicked it once, twice, three times, and the furrow-horse jumped up, trotted away triumphantly, and joyously rolled in the dam where all our water came from, drinking water included.

Dad went straight away to Smith's place, and told Smith he was a dirty, mean, despicable swindler—or something like that. Smith smiled. Dad put one leg through the slip-rails and promised Smith, if he'd only come along, to split palings out of him. But Smith didn't. The instinct of self-preservation must have been deep in that man Smith. Then Dad went home and said he would shoot the —— horse there and then, and went looking for the gun. The horse died in the paddock of old age, but Dad never ploughed with him again.

Dad followed the plough early and late. One day he was giving the horses a spell after some hours' work, when Joe came to say that a policeman was at the house wanting to see him. Dad thought of the roan mare, and Smith, and turned very pale. Joe said, "There's 'Q.P.' on his saddle-cloth. What's that for, Dad?" But he didn't answer—he was thinking hard. "And," Joe went on, "there's somethin' stickin' out of his pocket. Dave thinks it'll be 'an'cuffs."

Dad shuddered. On the way to the house Joe wished to speak about the policeman, but Dad seemed to have lock-jaw. When he found the officer of the law only wanted to know the number of stock he owned, he talked freely. He was delighted. He said, "Yes, sir," "No, sir," and "Jus' so, sir," to everything the policeman said.

Dad wished to learn some law. He said, "Now, tell me this. Supposing a horse gets into my paddock—or into your paddock—and I advertise that horse and nobody claims him, can't I put my brand on him?" The policeman jerked back his head and stared at the shingles long enough to recall all the robberies he had committed, and said, "Ye can—that's so—ye can."

"I knew it," answered Dad, "but a lawyer in town told Maloney, over there, y' couldn't."

"*Couldn't?*" And the policeman laughed till he nearly had the house down, only stopping to ask, while the tears ran over his well-fed cheeks, "Did he charge him forrit?"—and laughed again. He went away laughing, and for all I know the wooden-head may be laughing yet.

Everything was favourable to a good harvest. The rain fell just when it was wanted, and one could almost see the corn growing. How it encouraged Dad, and what new life it seemed to give him! In the cool of the evenings he would walk along the headlands and admire the forming cobs, and listen to the rustling of the rows of drooping blades as they swayed and beat against each other in the breeze. Then he would go home filled with fresh hopes and talk of nothing but the good prospect of that crop.

And how he worked! Joe was the only one who played. I remember his finding something on a chain one day. He had never seen anything like it before. Dad told him it was a steel trap and explained the working of it. Joe was entranced —an invaluable possession! A treasure, he felt, that the Lord must specially have sent him to catch things with. He caught many things with it—willie-wagtails, laughing jackasses, fowls, and mostly the dog. Joe was a born naturalist, a perfect McCooey in his way, and a close observer of the habits and customs of animals and living things. He observed that whenever Jacob Lipp came to our place he always, when going home, ran along the fence and touched the top of every post with his hand. The Lipps had newly arrived from Germany, and their selection adjoined ours. Jacob was their eldest, about fourteen, and a fat, jabbering, jolly faced youth. He often came to our place and followed Joe about. Joe never cared much for the company of anyone younger than himself, and therefore fiercely resented the indignity. Jacob could speak only German; Joe understood only pure unadulterated Australian. Still, Jacob insisted on talking and telling Joe his private affairs.

This day, Mrs Lipp accompanied Jacob. She came to have a yarn with Mother. They didn't understand each other either, but it didn't matter much to them. It never does matter much to women whether they understand or not. Anyway, they laughed most of the time and seemed to enjoy themselves greatly. Outside Jacob and Joe mixed up in an argument. Jacob shoved his face close to Joe's and gesticulated and talked German at the rate of two hundred words a minute. Joe thought he understood him and said, "You want to fight?" Jacob seemed to have a nightmare in German.

"Orright, then," Joe said, and knocked him down.

Jacob seemed to understand Australian better when he got up, for he ran inside, and Joe put his ear to a crack, but didn't hear him tell Mother.

Joe had an idea. He would set the steel trap on a wirepost and catch Jacob. He set it. Jacob started home. One, two, three posts he hit. Then he hit the trap. It grabbed him faithfully by three fingers.

Angels of Love! Did ever a boy of fourteen yell like it before! He sprang in the air, threw himself on the ground like a roped brumby, jumped up again and ran for all he knew, frantically wringing the hand the trap clung to. What Jacob reckoned had hold of him Heaven only can tell. His mother thought he must have gone mad and ran after him. Our Mother fairly tore after her. Dad and Dave left a dray-load of corn and joined in the hunt. Between them they got Jacob down and took him out of the trap. Dad smashed the infernal machine, and then went to look for Joe. But Joe wasn't about.

The corn shelled out a hundred bags—the best crop we had ever had. But when Dad came to sell, it seemed as though every farmer in every farming district on earth had had a heavy crop, for the market was glutted—there was too much corn in Egypt—and he could get no price for it. At last he was offered ninepence halfpenny per bushel, delivered at the railway station. Ninepence halfpenny per bushel, delivered at the railway station! Oh, my country! And fivepence per bushel out of that to a carrier to take it there! Australia, my mother!

Dad sold because he couldn't afford to await a better market. And when the letter came containing a cheque in payment, he made a calculation, then looked pitifully at Mother, and muttered, *"Seven pounds ten!"*

Chapter XII

KATE'S WEDDING

OUR selection was a great place for dancing. We could all dance, from Dan down, and there wasn't a figure or a movement we didn't know. We learnt young. Mother was a firm believer in early tuition. She used to say it was nice for young people to know how to dance, to be able to take their part when they went out anywhere, and not be awkward and stupid-looking when they went into society. It was awful, she thought, to see young fellows and big lumps of girls like the Bradys stalk into a ballroom and sit the whole night long in a corner, without attempting to get up. She didn't know how mothers *could* bring children up so ignorantly, and didn't wonder at some of them not being able to find husbands for their daughters.

But *we* had a lot to feel thankful for. Besides a sympathetic mother, every other facility was afforded us to become accomplished: abundance of freedom, enthusiastic sisters, and no matter how things were going—whether the corn wouldn't come up, or the wheat had failed, or the pumpkins had given out, or the waterhole run dry—we always had a concertina in the house. It never failed to attract company. Paddy Maloney and the well-sinkers, after belting and blasting all day long, used to drop in at night, and throw the table outside, and take the girls up, and prance about the floor with them till all hours.

Nearly every week Mother gave a ball. It might have been every night only for Dad. He said the jumping about destroyed the earth floor—wore it away and made the room like a well. And whenever it rained hard and the water rushed in *he* had to bail it out. Dad always looked on the dark side of things. He had no ear for music either. His want of appreciation of melody often made the home miserable when it might have been the merriest on earth. Sometimes it happened that he had to throw down the plough reins for half an hour or so to run round the wheat-paddock after a horse or an old cow. Then, if he found Dave, or Sal, or any of us sitting inside playing the concertina when he came to get a drink, he would nearly go mad.

"Can't y' find anything better t' do than everlastingly playing at that damn thing?" he would shout. And if we didn't put the instrument down immediately he would tear it from our hands and pitch it outside. If we *did* set it down quietly he would snatch it up and heave it out just as hard. The next evening he would devote all his time to patching the fragments together with sealing-wax.

Still, despite Dad's antagonism, we all turned out good players. It cost us nothing either. We learnt from each other. Kate was the first to learn. *She* taught Sal. Sal taught Dave, and so on. Sandy Taylor was Kate's tutor. He passed our place every evening going to his selection, where he used to sleep at night (fulfilling conditions), and always stopped at the fence to yarn with Kate about dancing. Sandy was a fine dancer himself, very light on his feet and easy to waltz with—so the girls made out. When the dancing subject was exhausted Sandy would drag some hair out of his horse's mane and say, "How's the concertina?" "It's in there," Kate would answer. Then turning round she would call out, "J—*oe*, bring the concer'."

In an instant Joe would strut along with it. And Sandy for the fiftieth time, would examine it and laugh at the kangaroo-skin straps that Dave had tacked to it, and the scraps of brown paper that were plastered over the ribs of it to keep the wind in; and, cocking his left leg over the pommel of his saddle, he would sound a full blast on it as a preliminary. Then he would strike up *The Rocky Road to Dublin*, or *The Wind Among the Barley*, or some other beautiful air, and grind away untiringly until it got dark—until Mother came and asked him if he wouldn't come in and have supper. Of course, he always would. After supper he would play some more. Then there would be a dance.

A ball was to be held at Anderson's one Friday night, and only Kate and Dave were asked from our place. Dave was very pleased to be invited; it was the first time he had been asked anywhere, and he began to practise vigorously. The evening before the ball Dad sent him to put the draught horses in the top paddock. He went off merrily with them. The sun was just going down when he let them go, and save the noise of the birds settling to rest the paddock was quiet. Dave was filled with emotion and enthusiastic thoughts about the ball. He threw the winkers down and looked around. For a moment or two he stood erect, then he bowed gracefully to the saplings on his right, then to the stumps and trees on his left, and humming a tune, ambled across a small patch of ground that was bare and black, and pranced back again. He opened his arms and, clasping some beautiful imaginary form in them, swung round and round like a windmill. Then he paused for breath, embraced his partner again, and "galloped" up and down. And young Johnson, who had been watching him in wonder from behind a fence, bolted for our place.

"Mrs Rudd! Mrs Rudd!" he shouted from the veranda. Mother went out.

"What's—what's up with Dave?"

Mother turned pale.

"There's *something*—!"

"My God!" Mother exclaimed. "Whatever has happened?"

Young Johnson hesitated. He was in doubt.

"Oh! What *is* it?" Mother moaned.

"Well—" he drew close to her, "—he's—he's *mad*!"

"*Oh-h!*"

"He *is*. I seen 'im just now up in your paddick, an' he's clean off he's pannikin."

Just then Dave came down the track whistling. Young Johnson saw him and fled.

For some time Mother regarded Dave with grave suspicion, then she questioned him closely.

"Yairs," he said, grinning hard, "I was goin' through the *fust set*."

It was when Kate was married to Sandy Taylor that we realized what a blessing it is to be able to dance. How we looked forward to that wedding! We were always talking about it, and were very pleased it would be held in our own house, because all of us could go then. None of us could work for thinking of it. Even Dad seemed to forget his troubles about the corn and Mick Brennan's threat to summons him for half the fence. Mother said we should want

71

plenty of water for the people to drink, so Sandy yoked his horse to the slide, and he, Dad, and Joe started for the springs.

The slide was the fork of a tree, alias a wheel-less water-trolly. The horse was hitched to the butt-end, and a batten nailed across the prongs kept the cask from slipping off going uphill. Sandy led the way and carried the bucket, Dad went ahead to clear the track of stones, and Joe straddled the cask to keep her steady.

It always took three to work the slide.

The water they brought was a little thick—old Anderson had been down and stirred it up pulling a bullock out— but Dad put plenty of ashes in the cask to clear it.

Each of us had his own work to do. Sandy knocked the partition down and decorated the place with boughs, Mother and the girls cooked and covered the walls with newspapers, and Dad gathered cow-dung and did the floor.

Two days before the wedding. All of us were still working hard. Dad was up to his armpits in a bucket of mixture, with a stack of cow-dung on one side, and a heap of sand and the shovel on the other. Dave and Joe were burning a cow that had died just in front of the house, and Sandy had gone to town for his tweed trousers.

A man in a long, black coat, white collar, and new leggings rode up, spoke to Dad, and got off. Dad straightened up and looked awkward, with his arms hanging wide and the mixture dripping from them. Mother came out. The cove shook hands with her, but he didn't with Dad. They went inside— not Dad, who washed himself first.

Dave sent Joe to ask Dad who the cove was. Dad spoke in a whisper and said he was Mr Macpherson, the clergyman who was to marry Kate and Sandy. Dave whistled and piled more wood on the dead cow. Mother came out and called Dave and Joe. Dave wouldn't go, but sent Joe.

Dave threw another log on the cow, then thought he would see what was going on inside.

He stood at the window and looked in. He couldn't believe his eyes at first, and put his head right in. There were Dad, Joe, and the lot of them down on their marrow-bones saying something after the parson. Dave was glad that he didn't go in.

How the parson prayed! Just when he said "Lead us not into temptation" the big kangaroo-dog slipped in and grabbed all the fresh meat on the table; but Dave managed to kick him in the ribs at the door. Dad groaned and seemed very restless.

When the parson had gone Dad said that what he had read about "reaping the same as you sow" was all rot, and spoke about the time when we sowed two bushels of barley in the lower paddock and got a big stack of rye from it.

The wedding was on a Wednesday, and at three o'clock in the afternoon. Most of the people came before dinner. The Hamiltons arrived just after breakfast. Talk of drays! The little paddock couldn't hold them.

Jim Mullins was the only one who came in to dinner; the others mostly sat on their heels in a row and waited in the shade of the wire fence. The parson was the last to come, and as he passed in he knocked his head against the kangaroo leg hanging under the veranda. Dad saw it swinging, and said angrily to Joe, "Didn't I tell you to take that down this morning?"

Joe unhooked it and said, "But if I hang it anywhere else the dog'll get it."

Dad tried to laugh at Joe and said loudly, "And what else is it for?" Then he bustled Joe off before he could answer him again.

Joe didn't understand.

Then Dad said, putting the leg in a bag, "Do you want

everyone to know we eat it, —— you?"

Joe understood.

The ceremony commenced. Those who could squeeze inside did so—the others looked in at the window and through the cracks in the chimney.

Mrs McDoolan led Kate out of the back room. Then Sandy rose from the fireplace and stood beside her. Everyone thought Kate looked very nice. And orange blossoms! You'd have thought she was an orange-tree with a new bed-curtain thrown over it. Sandy looked well, too, in his snake-belt and new tweeds, but he seemed uncomfortable when the pin that Dave had put in the back of his collar came out.

The parson didn't take long, and how they scrambled and tumbled over each other at the finish! Charley Mace said that he got the first kiss, Big George said *he* did, and Mrs McDoolan was certain she would have got it only for the baby.

Fun! There *was* fun! The room was cleared and they promenaded for a dance, Sandy and Kate in the lead. They continued promenading until one of the well-sinkers called

74

for the concertina—ours had been repaired till you could get only three notes out of it. But Jim Burke jumped on his horse and went home for his accordion.

Dance! They did dance—until sunrise! But unless you were dancing you couldn't stay inside, because the floor broke up. And talk about dust! Before morning the room was like a draughting-yard.

It was a great wedding, and all the neighbours used to say it was the best they were ever at.

Chapter XIII

THE SUMMER OLD BOB DIED

I T was a real scorcher. A soft, sweltering summer's day.
The air quivered; the heat drove the fowls under the
dray and sent the old dog to sleep upon the floor inside
the house. The iron on the skillion cracked and sweated, so
did Dad and Dave down the paddock, grubbing, grubbing,
in 130 degrees of sunshine. They were clearing a piece of
new land, a heavily timbered box-tree flat. They had been at
it a fortnight, and if any music had been in the ring of the
axe or the rattle of the pick when they started, there was
none now.

Dad wished to be cheerful and complacent. He said, putting the pick down and dragging his flannel off to wring it,
"It's a good thing to sweat well." Dave didn't say anything.
I don't know what he thought, but he looked up at Dad,
just looked up at him, while the sweat filled his eyes and ran
down over his nose like rain off a shingle, and then he
hitched up his pants and wired in again.

Dave was a philosopher. He worked away until the axe
flew off the handle with a ring and a bound, and might have
been lost in the long grass for ever only Dad stopped it with
his shin. I fancy he didn't mean to stop it when I think how
he jumped. It was the only piece of excitement there had
been the whole of that relentlessly solemn fortnight. Dad
got vexed—he was in a hurry with the grubbing—and said
he never could get anything done without something going
wrong. Dave wasn't sorry the axe came off—he knew it

meant half an hour in the shade fixing it on again. "Anyway," Dad went on, "we'll go to dinner now."

On the way to the house he several times looked at the sky—that cloudless, burning sky—and said, to no one in particular, "I wish to God it would rain!" It sounded like an aggravated prayer. Dave didn't speak, and I don't think Dad expected he would.

Joe was the last to sit down to dinner, and he came in steaming hot. He had chased out of sight a cow that had poked into the cultivation. Joe mostly went about with green bushes in his hat, to keep his head cool, and a few gum-leaves were now sticking in his moist and matted hair.

"I put her out, Dad," he said, casting an eager glance at everything on the table. "She tried to jump and got stuck on the fence, and broke it all down. On'y I couldn't get anything, I'd 'a' broke 'er 'ead—there wasn't a thing, on'y dead corn-stalks and cow-dung about." Then he lunged his fork desperately at a blowfly that persistently hovered about his plate, and commenced.

Joe had a healthy appetite. He had charged his mouth with a load of cold meat, when his jaws ceased work, and, opening his mouth as though he were sleepy, he leant forward and calmly returned it all to the plate. Dad got suspicious and asked Joe what was up, but Joe only wiped his mouth, looked sideways at his plate, and pushed it away.

All of us stopped eating then, and stared at each other. Mother said, "Well, I-I wrapped a cloth round it so nothing could get in, and put it in the safe. I don't know where on earth to put the meat, I'm sure. If I put it in a bag and hang it up that thief of a dog gets it."

"Yes," Dad observed, "I believe he'd stick his nose into hell itself, Ellen, if he thought there was a bone there—and there ought to be lots by this time." Then he turned over the remains of that cold meat, and, considering we had all witnessed the last kick of the slaughtered beast, it was surprising what animation this part of him yet retained. In vain did Dad explore for a really dead piece—there was life in all of it.

Joe wasn't satisfied. He said he knew where there were a lot of eggs, and disappeared down the yard. Eggs were not plentiful on our selection, because we too often had to eat the hens when there was no meat—three or four were as many as we ever saw at one time. So on this day, when Joe appeared with a hatful, there was excitement. He felt himself a hero. We thought him a little saviour.

"My!" said Mother. "Where did you get all those?"

"Get 'em? I've had these planted for three munce—they're a nest I found long ago. I thought I wouldn't say anything till we really wanted 'em."

Just then one of the eggs fell out of the hat and went off pop on the floor.

Dave nearly upset the table, he rose so suddenly, and covering his nose with one hand he made for the door. Then he scowled back over his shoulder at Joe. He utterly scorned his brother Joe. All of us deserted the table except Dad—he stuck to his place manfully. It took a lot to shift *him*.

Joe must have had a fine nerve. "That's on'y one bad 'n'," he said, taking the rest to the fireplace where the kettle stood. Then Dad, who had remained calm and majestic, broke out. "Damn y', boy!" he yelled. "Take th' awful things outside —you tinker!" Joe took them out and tried them all, but I forget if he found a good one.

Dad peered into the almost empty water-cask and again muttered a short prayer for rain. He decided to do no more grubbing that day, but to run wire around the new land instead. The posts had been in the ground some time, and had been bored. Dave and Sarah bored them. Sarah was as good as any man, so Dad reckoned. She could turn her hand to anything, from sewing a shirt to sinking a post-hole. She could give Dave inches in arm measurements, and talk about a leg! She *had* a leg—a beauty! It was as thick at the ankle as Dad's was at the thigh, nearly.

Anyone who wants to know what real amusement is should try wiring posts. What was to have been the top wire (the number 8 stuff) Dad commenced to put in the bottom holes, and we ran it through some twelve or fifteen posts before he saw the mistake. Then we dragged it out slowly and savagely, Dad swearing adequately all the time.

At last everything went splendidly. We dragged the wire through panel after panel, and at intervals Dad would examine the blistering sky for signs of rain. Once when he looked up a red bullock was reaching for his waistcoat, which hung on a branch of a low tree. Dad sang out. The bullock poked out his tongue and reached higher. Then Dad told Joe to run. Joe ran—so did the bullock, but faster, and with the waistcoat that once was a part of Mother's shawl half-way down his throat. Had the shreds and ribbons that dangled from it been a little longer, he might have trodden on them and pulled it back, but he didn't. Joe deemed it his duty to follow that red bullock till it dropped the waistcoat, so he hammered along full split behind. Dad and Dave stood watching until pursued and pursuer vanished down the gully. Then Dad said something about Joe being a fool, and they pulled at the wire again. They were nearing a corner post, and Dad was hauling the wire through the last panel, when there came the devil's own noise of galloping hoofs. Fifty or more cattle came careering along straight for the fence, bellowing and kicking up their heels in the air, as cattle do sometimes after a shower of rain. Joe was behind them—considerably—still at full speed and yelping like a dog. Joe loved excitement.

For weeks those cattle had been accustomed to go in and

79

out between the posts, and they didn't seem to have any thoughts of wire as they bounded along. Dave stood with gaping mouth. Dad groaned, and the wire-ends he was holding in his hand flew up with a whiz and took a scrap of his ear away. The cattle got mixed up in the wires. Some toppled over, some were caught by the legs, some by the horns. They dragged the wire twenty and thirty yards away, twisted it round logs, and left a lot of the posts pointing to sunset.

Oh, Dad's language then! He swung his arms about and foamed at the mouth. Dave edged away from him. Joe came up waving triumphantly a chewed piece of the waistcoat. "D-d-did it g-give them a buster, Dad?" he said, the sweat running over his face as though a spring had broken out on top of his head. Dad jumped a log and tried to unbuckle his strap and reach for Joe at the same time, but Joe fled.

That threw a painful pall over everything. Dad declared he was sick and tired of the whole thing, and wouldn't do another hand's turn. Dave mediated and walked along the fence, plucking off scraps of skin and hair that here and there clung to the bent and battered wire.

We had just finished supper when old Bob Wren, a bachelor who farmed about two miles from us, arrived. He used to come over every mail-night and bring his newspaper with him. Bob couldn't read a word, so he always got Dad to spell over the paper to him. *We* didn't take a newspaper.

Bob said there were clouds gathering behind Flat Top when he came in, and Dad went out and looked, and for the fiftieth time that day prayed in his own way for rain. Then he took the paper, and we gathered at the table to listen. "Hello," he commenced, "this is McDoolan's paper you've got, Bob."

Bob rather thought it wasn't.

"Yes, yes, man, it *is*," Dad put in. "See, it's addressed to him."

Bob leaned over and *looked* at the address, and said, "No, no, that's mine; it always comes like that." Dad laughed. We all laughed. He opened it, anyway. He hadn't read for five minutes when the light flickered nearly out. Sarah reckoned the oil was about done, and poured water in the lamp to raise the kerosene to the wick, but that didn't last long, and, as there was no fat in the house, Dad squatted on the floor and read by the firelight.

He plodded through the paper tediously from end to end, reading the murders and robberies a second time. The clouds that old Bob said were gathering when he came in were now developing to a storm, for the wind began to rise, and the giant ironbark-tree that grew close behind the house swayed and creaked weirdly, and threw out those strange sobs and moans that on wild nights bring terror to the hearts of bush children. A glimmer of lightning appeared through the cracks in the slabs. Old Bob said he would go before it came on, and started into the inky darkness.

"It's coming!" Dad said, as he shut the door and put the peg in after seeing old Bob out. And it came—in no time. A fierce wind struck the house. Then a vivid flash of lightning lit up every crack and hole, and a clap of thunder followed that nearly shook the place down.

Dad ran to the back door and put his shoulder against it, Dave stood to the front one, and Sarah sat on the sofa with her arms around Mother, telling her not to be afraid. The wind blew furiously; its one aim seemed the shifting of the house. Gust after gust struck the walls and left them quivering. The children screamed. Dad called and shouted, but no one could catch a word he said. Then there was one tremendous crack. We understood it—the ironbark-tree had gone over. At last, the shingled roof commenced to give.

Several times the ends rose (and our hair too) and fell back into place again with a clap. Then it went clean away in one piece, with a rip like a tearing ribbon, and there we stood, affrighted and shelterless, inside the walls. Then the wind went down and it rained—rained on us all night.

Next morning Joe had been to the new fence for the axe for Dad, and was off again as fast as he could run, when he remembered something and called out, "Dad, old B-B-Bob's just over there, lyin' down in the gully."

Dad started up. "It's 'im all right—I w-w-wouldn't 'a' noticed, only Prince s-s-smelt him."

"Quick and show me where!" Dad said.

Joe showed him.

"My God!" and Dad stood and stared. Old Bob it was—dead. Dead as Moses.

"Poor old Bob!" Dad said. "Poor—old—fellow!" Joe asked what could have killed him. "Poor—old—Bob!"

Dave brought the dray, and we took him to the house, or what remained of it.

Dad couldn't make out the cause of death; perhaps it was lightning. He held a post-mortem, and, after thinking hard for a long while, told Mother he was certain, anyway, that old Bob would never get up again. It was a change to have a dead man about the place, and we were very pleased to be first to tell anyone who didn't know the news about old Bob.

We planted him on his own selection beneath a gum-tree where for years and years a family of jackasses had nightly roosted, Dad remarking, "As there *might* be a chance of his hearin', it'll be company for the poor old cove."

Chapter XIV

WHEN DAN CAME HOME

Oᴺᴇ night after the threshing. Dad lying on the sofa, thinking, the rest of us sitting at the table. Dad spoke to Joe.

"How much," he said, "is seven hundred bushels of wheat at six shillings?"

Joe, who was looked upon as the brainy one of our family, took down his slate with a hint of scholarly ostentation.

"What did y' say, Dad—seven 'undred *bags?*"

"Bushels! *Bushels!*"

"Seven 'un-dered bush-els of wheat. *Wheat* was it, Dad?"

"Yes, *wheat!*"

"Wheat at. . . . At *what*, Dad?"

"Six shillings a bushel."

"Six shil-lings a. . . . *A*, Dad? We've not done any at *a*; she's on'y showed us *per!*"

"*Per* bushel, then!"

"Per bush-el. That's seven 'undred bushels of wheat at six shillin's per bushel. An' y' wants ter know, Dad—?"

"How much it'll be, of course."

"In money, Dad, or—er—?"

"Dammit, yes. *Money!*" Dad raised his voice.

For a while, Joe thought hard, then set to work figuring and rubbing out, figuring and rubbing out. The rest of us eyed him, envious of his learning.

Joe finished the sum.

"Well?" from Dad.

Joe cleared his throat. We listened.

"Nine thousan' poun'."

Dave laughed loud. Dad said, "Pshaw!"—and turned his face to the wall. Joe looked at the slate again.

"Oh! I see," he said, "I didn't divide by twelve t' bring t' pounds", and laughed himself.

More figuring and rubbing out.

Finally Joe, in loud, decisive tones, announced, "*Four* thousand, *no* 'undred an' twenty poun', fourteen shillin's an'—"

"Bah! *You* blockhead!" Dad blurted out, and jumped off the sofa and went to bed.

We all turned in.

We were not in bed long when the dog barked and a horse entered the yard. There was a clink of girth-buckles; a saddle was thrown down; then a thump, as though with a lump of blue-metal, set the dog yelping lustily. We lay listening till a voice called out at the door, "All in bed?" Then we knew it was Dan, and Dad and Dave sprang out in their shirts to let him in. All of us jumped up to see Dan. This time he had been away a long while, and when the slush-lamp was lit and fairly going, how we stared and wondered at his altered looks! He had grown a long whisker, and must have stood inches higher than Dad.

Dad was delighted. He put a fire on, made tea, and he and Dan talked till near daybreak, Dad of the harvest, and the government dam that was promised, and the splendid grass growing in the paddock, Dan of the great dry plains, and the shearing-sheds outback, and the chaps he had met there. And he related in a way that made Dad's eyes glisten and Joe's mouth open, how, with a knocked-up wrist, he shore beside Proctor and big Andy Purcell, at Welltown, and rung the shed by half a sheep.

Dad ardently admired Dan.

Dan was only going to stay a short while at home, he said, then was off west again. Dad tried to persuade him to change his mind; he would have him remain and help to work the selection. But Dan only shook his head and laughed.

Dan accompanied Dad to the plough every morning, and walked cheerfully up and down the furrows all day, talking to him. Sometimes he took a turn at the plough, and Dad did the talking. Dad just loved Dan's company.

A few days went by. Dan still accompanied Dad to the plough, but didn't walk up and down with him. He selected a shade close by, and talked to Dad from there as he passed on his rounds. Sometimes Dan used to forget to talk at all—he would be asleep—and Dad would wonder if he was unwell. Once he advised him to go up to the house and have a good camp. Dan went. He stretched himself on the sofa and smoked and spat on the floor and played the concertina—an old one he won in a raffle.

Dan didn't go near the plough any more. He stayed inside every day, and drank the yeast, and provided music for the women. Sometimes he would leave the sofa, and go to the back door and look out, and watch Dad tearing up and down the paddock after the plough. Then he'd yawn, and wonder aloud what the diggins it was the old man saw in a game like that on a hot day, and return to the sofa, tired. But every evening when Dad knocked off and brought the horses to the barn Dan went out and watched him un-harnessing them.

A month passed. Dad wasn't so fond of Dan now, and Dan never talked of going away. One day Anderson's cows wandered into our yard and surrounded the haystack. Dad saw them from the paddock and cooeed, and shouted for those at the house to drive them away. They didn't hear him. Dad left the plough and ran up and pelted Anderson's cows with stones and glass bottles, and pursued them with a

85

pitch-fork till, in a mad rush to get out, half the brutes fell over the fence and made havoc with the wire. Dad spent an hour mending it, then went to the veranda and savagely asked Mother if she had lost her ears. Mother said she hadn't. "Then why the devil couldn't y' hear me singin' out?" Mother thought it must have been because Dan was playing the concertina. "Oh, *damn* his concertina!" Dad squealed, and kicked Joe's little kitten, which was rubbing itself fondly against his leg, clean through the house.

Dan found the selection pretty slow—so he told Mother—and thought he would knock about a bit. He went to the store and bought a supply of ammunition, which he booked to Dad, and started shooting. He stood at the door and put twenty bullets into the barn. Then he shot two bears near the stock-yard with twenty more bullets, and dragged both bears down to the house and left them at the back door. They stayed at the back door until they went very bad; then Dad hooked himself to them and dragged them down the gully.

Somehow, Dad began to hate Dan. He scarcely ever spoke to him now, and at meal-times never spoke to any of us. Dad was a hard man to understand. *We* couldn't understand him. "And with *Dan* at home, too!" Sal used to whine. Sal verily idolized Dan. Hero-worship was strong in Sal.

One night Dad came in for supper rather later than usual. He'd had a hard day, and was done up. To make matters worse, when he was taking the collar off Captain the brute tramped heavily on his toe, and took the nail off. Supper wasn't ready. The dining-room was engaged. Dan was showing Sal how the Prince of Wales schottische was danced in the huts outback. For music, Sal was humming, and the two were flying about the room. Dad stood at the door and looked on with blood in his eye.

"Look here," he thundered suddenly, interrupting Dan, "I've had enough of you!" The couple stopped, astonished, and Sal cried, "*Dad!*" But Dad was hot. "Out of this!"—placing his hand on Dan, and shoving him. "You've loafed long enough on me! Off y' go t' the devil!"

Dan went over to Anderson's and Anderson took him in and kept him a week. Then Dan took Anderson down at a new game of cards, and went away west again.

Chapter XV

OUR CIRCUS

Dave had been to town and came home full of circus. He sat on the ground beside the tubs while Mother and Sal were washing, and raved about the riding and the tumbling he had seen. He talked enthusiastically to Joe about it every day for three weeks. Dave rose very high in Joe's estimation.

Raining. All of us inside. Sal on the sofa playing the concertina; Dad squatting on the edge of a flat stone at the corner of the fireplace, Dave on another opposite, both gazing into the fire, which was almost out, and listening intently to the music; the dog, dripping wet, coiled at their feet, shivering; Mother sitting dreamily at the table, her palm pressed against her cheek, also enjoying the music.

Sal played on until the concertina broke. Then there was a silence.

For a while Dave played with a piece of charcoal. At last he spoke. "Well," he said, looking at Dad, "what about this circus?"

Dad chuckled.

"But what d' y' *think*?"

"Well—" Dad paused—"yes—" chuckled again—"very well."

"A *circus*!" Sal put in. "A pretty circus yous'd have!"

Dave fired up. "*You* go and ride the red heifer, strad-legs, same as y' did yesterday," he snarled, "an' let all the country see y'."

Sal blushed.

Then to Dad, "I'm certain, with Paddy Maloney in it, we could do it right enough, and make it pay, too."

"Very well, then," said Dad. "Very well. There's the tarpaulin there, and plenty bales and old bags whenever you're ready."

Dave was delighted, and he and Dad and Joe ran out to see where the tent could be pitched, and ran in again wetter than the dog.

One day a circus tent went up in our yard. It attracted a lot of notice. Two of the Johnsons and old Anderson and others rode in on draught-horses and inspected it. And Smith's spring-cart horse, which used to be driven by every day, stopped in the middle of the lane and stared at it, and when Smith stood up and belted him with the double of the reins, he bolted and upset the cart over a stump. It wasn't a very white tent. It was made of bags and green bushes, and Dad and Dave and Paddy Maloney were two days putting it up.

We all assisted in the preparations for the circus. Dad built seats out of forked sticks and slabs, and Joe gathered jam tins which Mother filled with fat and moleskin wicks to light up with.

Everyone in the district knew about our circus, and longed for the opening night. It came. A large fire near the slip-rails, shining across the lane and lighting up a corner of the wheat-paddock, showed the way in.

Dad stood at the door to take the money. The Andersons —eleven of them—arrived first. They didn't walk straight in. They hung about for a while. Then Anderson sidled up to Dad and talked into his ear. "Oh, that's all right," Dad said, and passed them all in without taking any money.

Next came the Maloneys, and, as Paddy belonged to the

circus, they also walked in without paying, and secured front seats.

Then Jim Brown, and Sam Holmes, and Walter Nutt, and Steve Burton, and eight others strolled along. Dad owed all of them money for binding, which they happened to remember. "In you go," Dad said, and in the lot went. The tent filled quickly, and the crowd awaited the opening act.

Paddy Maloney came forward with his hair oiled and combed, and rang the cow bell.

Dave, bare-footed and bare-headed, in snow-white moles and red shirt, entered standing majestically upon old Ned's back. He got a great reception. But Ned was tired and refused to canter. He jogged lazily round the ring. Dave shouted at him and rocked about. He was very unsteady. Paddy Maloney flogged Ned with the leg-rope. But Ned had been flogged often before. He got slower and slower. Suddenly, he stood and cocked his tail, and to prevent himself falling, Dave jumped off. Then the audience yelled while Dave dragged Ned into the dressing-room and punched him on the nose.

Paddy Maloney made a speech. He said, "Well, the next item on the programme'll knock y' bandy. Keep quiet, you fellows, now, an' y'll see somethin'."

They saw Joe. He stepped backwards into the ring, pulling at a string. There was something on the string. "Come on!" Joe said, tugging. The "something" wouldn't come. "Chuck 'im in!" Joe called out. Then the pet kangaroo was heaved in through the doorway, and fell on its head and raised the dust. A great many ugly dogs rushed for it savagely. The kangaroo jumped up and bounded round the ring. The dogs pursued him noisily. "*Gerrout!*" Joe shouted, and the crowd stood up and became very enthusiastic. The dogs caught the kangaroo, and were dragging him to earth when Dad rushed in and kicked them in twos to the top of the tent. Then, while Johnson expostulated with Dad for laming his brindle slut, the kangaroo dived through a hole in the tent and rushed into the house and into the bedroom, and sprang on the bed among a lot of babies and women's hats.

When the commotion subsided Paddy Maloney rang the cow bell again, and Dave and Podgy, the pet sheep, rode out on Nugget. Podgy sat with hind-legs astride the horse and his head leaning back against Dave's chest. Dave (standing up) bent over him with a pair of shears in his hand. He was to shear Podgy as the horse cantered round.

Paddy Maloney touched Nugget with the whip, and off he went, "rump-ti-dee, dump-ti-dee." Dave rolled about a lot the first time round, but soon got his equilibrium. He brandished the shears and plunged the points of them into Podgy's belly-wool, also into Podgy's skin. "Bur-*ur-r*!" Podgy blurted and struggled violently. Dave began to topple about. He dropped the shears. The audience guffawed. Then Dave jumped, but Podgy's horns got caught in his clothes and made trouble. Dave hung on one side of the horse and the sheep dangled on the other. Dave sang out, so did Podgy. And the horse stopped and snorted, then swung furiously round and round until five or six pairs of hands seized his head and held him.

Dave didn't repeat the act. He ran away holding his clothes together.

It was a very successful circus. Everyone enjoyed it and wished to see it again—everyone but the Maloneys. *They* said it was a swindle, and ran Dad down because he didn't divide with Paddy the three and sixpence he took at the door.

Chapter XVI

WHEN JOE WAS IN CHARGE

JOE was a naturalist. He spent a lot of time, time that Dad considered should have been employed cutting burr or digging potatoes, in ear-marking bears and bandi-coots, and catching goannas and letting them go without their tails, or coupled in pairs with pieces of greenhide. The paddock was full of goannas in harness and slit-eared bears. They belonged to Joe.

Joe also took an interest in snakes, and used to poke amongst logs and brush fences in search of rare specimens. Whenever he secured a good one he put it in a cage and left it there until it died or got out, or Dad threw it, cage and all, right out of the parish.

One day, while Mother and Sal were out with Dad, Joe came home with a four-foot black snake in his hand. It was a beauty. So sleek and lithe and lively! He carried it by the tail, its head swinging close to his bare leg, and the thing yearning for a grab at him. But Joe understood the ways of a reptile.

There was no cage—Dad had burnt the last one—so Joe walked round the room wondering where to put his prize. The cat came out of the bedroom and mewed and followed him for the snake. He told her to go away. She didn't go. She reached for the snake with her paw. It bit her. She spat and sprang in the air and rushed outside with her back up. Joe giggled and wondered how long the cat would live.

The Rev. Macpherson, on his way to christen McKenzie's baby, called in for a drink, and smilingly asked after Joe's health.

"Hold this kuk-kuk-cove, then," Joe said, handing the parson the reptile, which was wriggling and biting at space, "an' I'll gug-gug-get y' one." But when Mr Macpherson saw the thing was alive he jumped back and fell over the dog which was lying behind him in the shade. Bluey grabbed him by the leg, and the parson jumped up in haste and made for his horse, followed by Bluey. Joe cried, "*Come* 'ere!"— then turned inside.

Mother and Sal entered. They had come to make Dad and themselves a cup of tea. They quarrelled with Joe, and he went out and started playing with the snake. He let it go, and went to catch it by the tail again, but the snake caught *him*—by the finger.

"He's bit me!" Joe cried, turning pale. Mother screeched, and Sal bolted off for Dad, while the snake glided silently up the yard.

Anderson, passing on his old bay mare, heard the noise and came in. He examined Joe's finger, bled the wound, and was bandaging the arm when Dad rushed in.

"Where is he?" he said. "Oh, you damned whelp! You wretch of a boy! My God!"

" 'Twasn' *my* fault." And Joe began to blubber.

But Anderson protested. There was no time, he said, to be lost barneying; and he told Dad to take his old mare Jean and go at once for Sweeney. Sweeney was the publican at Kangaroo Creek, with a reputation for curing snake-bite. Dad ran out, mounted Jean, and turned her head for Sweeney's. But, at the slip-rails, Jean stuck him up, and wouldn't go farther. Dad hit her between the ears with his fist, and got down and ran back.

"The boy'll be dead, Anderson," he cried, rushing inside again.

"Come on, then," Anderson said, "we'll take off his finger."

Joe was looking drowsy. But, when Anderson took hold of him and placed the wounded finger on a block, and Dad faced him with the hammer and a blunt, rusty old chisel, he livened up.

"No, Dad, no!" he squealed, straining and kicking like an old man kangaroo. Anderson stuck to him, though, and with Sal's assistance held his finger on the block till Dad carefully rested the chisel on it and brought the hammer down. It didn't sever the finger—it only scraped the nail off—but it *did* make Joe buck. He struggled desperately and got away.

Anderson couldn't run at all; Dad was little faster; Sal could run like a greyhound in her bare feet, but, before she could pull her boots off, Joe had disappeared in the corn.

"Quick!" Dad shouted, and the trio followed the patient. They hunted through the corn from end to end, but found no trace of him. Night came. The search continued. They called, and called, but nothing answered save the ghostly echoes, the rustling of leaves, the slow, sonorous notes of a distant bear, or the neighing of a horse in the grass-paddock.

At midnight they gave up, and went home, and sat inside and listened and looked distracted.

While they sat, Whisky, a blackfellow from Billson's station, dropped in. He was taking a horse down to town for his boss, and asked Dad if he could stay till morning. Dad said he could. He slept in Dave's bed. Dave slept on the sofa.

"If Joe ain't dead, and wuz t' come in before mornin'," Dave said, "there won't be room for us all."

And before morning Joe did come in. He entered stealthily by the back door, and crawled quietly into bed.

At daybreak Joe awoke, and nudged his bed-mate and said, "Dave, the cocks has crowed!" No answer. He nudged him again.

"Dave, the hens is all off the roost!" Still no reply.

Daylight streamed in through the cracks. Joe sat up—he was at the back—and stared about. He glanced at the face of his bedmate and chuckled and said, "Who's been blackenin' y', Dave?"

He sat grinning awhile, then stood up, and started pulling on his trousers, which he drew from under his pillow. He had put one leg into them when his eyes rested on a pair of black feet uncovered at the foot of the bed. He stared at them and the black face again—then plunged for the door and fell. Whisky was awake and grinned over the side of the bed at him.

"What makit you so frightent like that?" he said, grinning more.

Joe ran into Mother's room and dived in behind her and Dad. Dad swore, and kicked Joe and jammed him against the slabs with his heels, saying, "My *Gawd*! You *devil* of a feller, how (*kick*) dare you (*kick*) run (*kick*) run (*kick, kick, kick*) away yesterday, eh?" (*kick*).

But he was very glad to see Joe all the same. We all felt that Shingle Hut would not have been the same place at all without Joe.

It was when Dad and Dave were away after kangaroo

95

scalps that Joe was most appreciated. Mother and Sal felt it such a comfort to have a man in the house, even if it was only Joe.

Joe was proud of his male prerogatives. He looked after the selection, minded the corn, kept Anderson's and Dwyer's and Brown's and old Mother Murphy's cows out of it, and chased goannas away from the front door the same as Dad used to do—for Joe felt that he was in Dad's place, and postponed his customary familiarities with the goannas.

It was while Joe was in charge that Casey came to our place. A starved-looking, toothless little old man with a restless eye, talkative, ragged and grey, he walked with a bend in his back (not a hump), and carried his chin in the air. We had never seen a man like him before. He spoke rapidly, too, and watched us all as he talked. Not exactly a traveller, he carried no swag or billycan, and wore a pair of boots much too large. He seemed to have been well brought up—he took off his hat at the door and bowed low to Mother and Sal, who were sitting inside, sewing. They gave a start and stared. The dog, lying at Mother's feet, rose and growled. Bluey wasn't used to the ways of people well brought up.

The world had dealt harshly with Casey, and his story went to Mother's heart. "God buless y'," he said when she told him he could have some dinner, "but I'll cut y' wood for it. Oh, I'll cut y' wood!" And he went to the woodheap and started work. A big heap and a blunt axe, but it didn't matter to Casey. He worked hard, and didn't stare about, and didn't reduce the heap much, either; and when Sal called him to dinner he couldn't hear—he was too busy. Joe had to go and bring him away.

Casey sat at the table and looked up at the holes in the roof, through which the sun was shining.

"Ought t' be a cool house," he remarked.

Mother said it was.

"Quite a bush house."

"Oh, yes," Mother said, "we're right in the bush here."

He began to eat and, as he ate, talked cheerfully of selections and crops and old times and bad times and wire fences and dead cattle. Casey was a versatile ancient. When he was finished he shifted to the sofa and asked Mother how many children she had. Mother considered and said, "Twelve." He thought a dozen enough for anyone, and, said that *his* mother, when he left home, had twenty-one—all girls but him. That was forty years ago, and he didn't know how many she'd had since. Mother and Sal smiled. They began to like old Casey.

Casey took up his hat and went outside, and didn't say "good day" or "thanks" or anything. He didn't go away, either. He looked about the yard. A panel in the fence was broken. It had been broken for five years. Casey seemed to know it. He started mending that panel. He was mending it all the evening.

Mother called to Joe to bring in some wood. Casey left the fence, hurried to the woodheap, carried in an armful, and asked Mother if she wanted more. Then he returned to the fence.

"J-*oe*," Mother screeched a little later, "look at those cows tryin' to eat the corn."

Casey left the fence again and drove the cows away, and mended the wire on his way back.

At sundown Casey was cutting more wood, and when we were at supper he brought it in and put some on the fire, and went out again slowly.

Mother and Sal talked about him. "Better give him his supper," Sal said, and Mother sent Joe to invite him in. He didn't come in at once. Casey wasn't a forward man. He stayed to throw some pumpkin to the pigs.

Casey slept in the barn that night. He slept in it the next night, too. He didn't believe in shifting from place to place, so he stayed with us altogether. He took a lively interest in the selection. The house, he said, was in the wrong place, and he showed Mother where it ought to have been built. He suggested shifting it, and setting a hedge and ornamental trees in front and fruit-trees at the back, and making a nice place of it. Little things like that pleased Mother. "Anyway," she would sometimes say to Sal, "he's a useful old man, and knows how to look after things about the place." Casey did. Whenever any water-melons were ripe, he looked after them and hid the skins in the ground. And if a goanna or a crow came and frightened a hen from her nest Casey always got the egg, and when he had gobbled it up he would chase that crow or goanna for its life and shout lustily.

Every day saw Casey more at home at our place. He was a very kind man and most obliging. If a traveller called for a drink of water, Casey would give him a cup of milk and ask him to wait and have dinner. If Maloney or old Anderson or anybody wished to borrow a horse or a dray or anything about the place, Casey would let them have it with pleasure, and tell them not to be in a hurry about returning it.

Joe got on well with Casey. Casey's views on hard work were the same as Joe's. Hard work, Joe thought, wasn't necessary on a selection.

Casey knew a thing or two, so he said. One fine morning, when all the sky was blue and the butcher-birds whistling strong, Dwyer's cows smashed down a lot of the fence and dragged it into the corn. Casey, assisted by Joe, put them all in the yard, and hammered them with sticks. Dwyer came along.

"Those cattle belong to me," he said angrily.

"They belongs t' *me*," Casey answered, "until you pay damages." Then he put his back to the slip-rails and looked up aggressively into Dwyer's face. Dwyer was a giant beside Casey. Dwyer didn't say anything—he wasn't a man of words—but started throwing the rails down to let the cows out. Casey flew at him. Dwyer quietly shoved him away with his long, brown arm. Casey came again and fastened on to Dwyer. Joe mounted the stock-yard. Dwyer seized Casey with both hands; then there was a struggle, on Casey's part. Dwyer lifted him up and carried him away and set him down on his back, then hastened to the rails. But before he could throw them down Casey was upon him again. Casey never knew when he was beaten. Dwyer was getting annoyed. He took Casey by the back of the neck and squeezed him. Casey humped his shoulders and gasped. Dwyer stared about. A plough-rein hung on the yard. Dwyer reached for it. Casey yelled, "Murder!" Dwyer fastened one end of the rope round Casey's body—under the arms— and stared about again. And again "Murder!" from Casey. Joe jumped off the yard to get farther away. A tree with a high horizontal limb stood near. Dad had once used it as a butcher's gallows. Dwyer gathered the loose rein into a coil and heaved it over the limb, and hauled Casey up. Then he tied the end of the rope to the yard and drove out the cows.

"When y' want 'im down," Dwyer said to Joe as he walked away, "cut the rope."

Casey groaned, and one of his boots dropped off. Then he began to spin round—to wind up and unwind and wind up again. Joe came near and eyed the twirling form with joy.

Mother and Sal arrived, breathless and excited. They screeched at Joe.

"Undo the r-r-rope," Joe said, "an' he'll come w-w-wop."

Sal ran away and procured a sheet, and Mother and she held it under Casey, and told Joe to unfasten the rope and lower him as steadily as he could. Joe unfastened the rope, but somehow it pinched his fingers and he let go, and Casey fell through the sheet. For three weeks Casey was an invalid at our place. He would have been invalided there for the rest of his days only old Dad came home and induced him to leave. Casey didn't want to go, but Dad had a persuasive way with him that generally proved effectual.

Singularly enough, Dad complained that kangaroos were getting scarce where he was camped, while our paddocks were full of them. Joe started a mob nearly every day, as he walked round overseeing things, and he pondered. Suddenly he had an original inspiration—originality was Joe's strong point. He turned the barn into a workshop, and buried himself there for two days. For two whole days he was never "at home", except when he stepped out to throw the hammer at the dog for yelping for a drink. The greedy brute! It wasn't a week since he'd had a billyful, Joe told him. On the morning of the third day the barn door swung open, and forth came a kangaroo, with a sharpened carving knife in its paws. It hopped across the yard and sat up, bold and erect, near the dog kennel. Bluey nearly broke his neck trying to get at it. The kangaroo said, "Lay down, you useless hound!"—and started across the cultivation, heading for the grass-paddock in long, erratic jumps. Half-way across the cultivation it spotted a mob of other kangaroos, and took a firmer grip of the carver.

Bluey howled and plunged until Mother came out to see what was the matter. She was in time to see a solitary kangaroo hop in a drunken manner towards the fence, so she let the dog go and cried, "Sool him, Bluey! Sool him!" Bluey sooled him, and Mother followed with the axe to get the scalp. As the dog came racing up, the kangaroo turned and hissed, "G' home, y' mongrel!" Bluey took no notice, and only when he had nailed the kangaroo dextrously by the thigh and got him down did it dawn upon the marsupial that Bluey wasn't in the secret. Joe tore off his head-gear, called the dog affectionately by name, and yelled for help. But Bluey had not had anything substantial to eat for over a week, and he worried away vigorously.

Then the kangaroo slashed out with the carving knife, and hacked a junk off Bluey's nose. Bluey shook his head, relaxed his thigh-grip, and grabbed the kangaroo by the ribs. How that kangaroo did squeal! Mother arrived. She dropped the axe, threw up both hands, and shrieked. "Pull him off! He's eating me!" gasped the kangaroo. Mother shrieked louder, and wrung her hands, but it had no effect on Bluey. He was a good dog, was Bluey!

At last, Mother got him by the tail and dragged him off, but he took a mouthful of kangaroo with him as he went. Then the kangaroo raised itself slowly on to its hands and knees. It was very white and sick-looking, and Mother threw her arms round it and cried, "Oh, Joe, my child, my child!"

It was several days before Joe felt better. When he did, Bluey and he went down the gully together and, after a while, Joe came back—like Butler—alone.

I

Our New Selection

Chapter I

BAPTIZING BARTHOLOMEW

THE baby, twelve months old, was to be christened, and Mother decided to give a party. She had been thinking about the party for some time, but decision was contemporaneous with the arrival of a certain mysterious parcel. We were preparing for the christening. Dad and Dave drawing water; Joe raking husks and corn-cobs into a heap at the door and burning them; Little Bill collecting the pumpkins and pie-melons strewn about the yard. Mother and Sal were busy inside. Mother stood on a box. Sal spread newspapers on the table and smeared them over with paste, then handed them cautiously to Mother, who fixed them on the wall. The baby crawled on the floor.

"Not that way," said Mother. "That's upside down. Give them to me straight, 'cause your father sometimes likes to read them when they're up."

They chatted about the christening.

"Indeed, then, she won't be asked," Sal said. "Not if she goes down on her knees, the skinny little ——"

"Min', min', mind, girl!" Mother screeched, and Sal dropped the newspaper she was about to hand up, and, jumping a stool, caught the baby by the skirt-tail just as it was about to wobble into the fire.

"My goodness! You little rat!" The baby laughed playfully and struggled to get out of her arms. Sal placed it at the opposite side of the room and the decorating continued.

"I can remember the time, then," Mother said, "when they hadn't so much to be flash about, when the old woman and that eldest girl, Johanna, used to go about in their bare feet and with dresses on—dear me—that I wouldn't give a black-gin!"

"Not Johanna, Mother?"

"Yes. Johanna. You wouldn't remember it, of course. Norah was the baby then."

"You little wretch!" And Sal rushed for the baby and pulled it from the fire once more. She dumped it down in a different corner, and returned to the paste. The baby made eagerly for the fire again, but when half-way across the room it stopped, rested its cheek on the floor and fell asleep —and it on the verge of being christened Bartholomew— until Dad came in and took it up.

Mother went into her bedroom and came out with a flaring red sash flying over her greasy gown, and asked Dad if he liked it. Dad looked at the ribbon, then out of the window and chuckled.

"What d'y' think of me?"

"Think of y'?" And Dad grinned.

Mother looked fondly at the ribbon. She was very satisfied with herself. She was a true woman, was Mother. She tripped into the room again and came out with some yards of print, and asked Dad what he thought of that. Mother was fond of dress.

"Dear me, woman," Dad said, "what's going to happen?"

"But how do y' like it?"—letting it hang like a skirt.

Dad grinned more.

"Is it a nice pattern?"

Dad still grinned.

"Does it suit me?"

Dad looked out the window and saw Joe knock Little Bill down with a pumpkin. He ran out.

"Men haven't a bit of taste," Mother said to Sal, folding the print, "except just for what—" Joe rushed in at the front door and out at the back one—" 'cept for what's to go in their stomachs. All they think about's an old—" Dad rushed in at the front door and out the back one—"old horse or something. And then they think—" Joe rushed in again at the front door, but dived under the sofa—"think every old screw is a race-horse—" Dad rushed in again at the front door and out at the back one. "My word, if he finds you there, me shaver, y'll catch it!"

Joe grinned and breathed hard.

Mother put the print away and mounted the box again. Then Mrs Flannigan, a glib-tongued old gossip, the mother of sixteen shy selector children, dropped in, and they drank tea together and talked about christenings and matches and marriages and babies and bad times and bad husbands until dark—until Mrs Flannigan thought her husband would be wanting his supper and went home.

Joe talked of the christening at school. For a time nobody paid any attention to him; but as days passed and one and another went home to find that mother and father and bigger brothers and sisters had been asked, the interest grew, and a revulsion of feeling in favour of Joe set in. First Nell Anderson suddenly evinced a desire for his society—previously she would weep if made stand next him in class. Then the Murphys and the Browns and young Roberts surrounded him, and Reuben Burton put his string bridle on him and wouldn't ride any other horse in a race, till at last Joe became the idol of the institution. They all fawned on him and followed him about—all but the two Caseys. They were isolated, and seemed to feel their position keenly.

Joe was besieged with questions and answered them all with a head-shake and a snuffling of one nostril. He disclosed all the arrangements and gave melting descriptions of the pies and puddings Mother was preparing. How they danced round him and called him "Joseph"! The two Caseys stood off in silence, and in fancy saw those pies and puddings— a pleasant contemplation till Nell Anderson pointed to them and asked Joe if they were invited.

"Nah," Joe said, "n-n-none of 'em is."

"Ain't their mother?"

"N-nah, we d-don't want 'em", and he snuffled more. Then the two Caseys stole away to the rear of the school, where they sat and nursed their chagrin in lugubrious silence, and caught flies mechanically, and looked down at their dusty bare feet over which the ants crawled, until the teacher thumped the end of the little building with a huge paling and school went in.

The day came, and we all rose early and got ready. The parson, who had to ride twenty-five miles to be present, came about midday. His clothes were dusty, and he looked tired. Mother and Sal wondered if they should offer him something to eat or let him wait until the guests arrived and all sat down to the big spread. They called Dad and Dave into the little tumble-down kitchen to discuss the matter. Dad said he didn't care what they did, but Dave settled it. He said, "Get the chap a feed."

Joe sat on the sofa beside the parson's tall hat and eyed it in wonder. Joe had never seen so much respectability before. The parson ate with his back turned to Joe, while Mother and Sal flew busily about. Joe cautiously put out his hand to feel the beaver. Mother saw him and frowned. Joe withdrew his hand and stared at the rafters.

"Delicious tea," said the parson, and Mother served him with more.

Joe's hand stole out to the hat again. Dave, standing outside near the front door, noticed him and grinned. That emboldened Joe, and he lifted the hat and placed his head inside it and grinned out at Dave. Mother frowned more, but Joe couldn't see her. She hurried out. Then from the back of the house Dad's voice thundered, "Joe!" Joe removed the beaver and obeyed the call. Harsh, angry whispers came from the door, then sounds of a scuffle, and an empty bucket flew after Joe as he raced across the yard towards the haystack.

Soon the guests began to arrive. The Maloneys and the Todds and the Taits and the Thomsons and others, with children and dogs, came in spring-carts and drays from Back Creek. The Watsons and the Whites and old Holmes and Judy Jubb, from Prosperity Peak, appeared on horseback. Judy, in the middle of the yard, stepped out of a torn and tattered old riding habit, with traces of the cow-yard about it, and displayed a pair of big boots and "railway" stockings and a nice white muslin dress with red bows and geraniums and a lot of frills and things on it. Judy was very genteel.

The Sylvesters—nice people who had come from Brisbane with new ideas and settled near us, people who couldn't leg-rope a cow, who were going to make a big thing out of fowls, who were for ever asking Dad if jew-lizards were snakes—came on foot with their baby in a little painted cart. A large black dog, well groomed and in new harness, without reins, pulled the cart along.

We had never seen a dog pulling a cart before, neither had our dog. He rushed off to meet the Sylvesters, but stopped half-way and curled his tail over his back and growled and threw earth about with his legs. The Sylvesters' dog stood also, and curled his tail over his harness. Mrs Sylvester patted him and said, "Carlo, Carlo, you naughty boy!"

Our dog suddenly made off. The Sylvesters' dog pursued him. He tore along the fence at coursing speed, making a great noise with the cart until he turned a corner, where it upset and left the baby. But he didn't catch our dog. And Paddy Maloney and Steve Burton and young Wilkie galloped up through the paddock shouting and whipping their horses and carried away the clothes-line stretched between two trees at the back.

The house soon filled—there was just room for big Mrs McDoolan to squeeze in. She came on foot, puffing and blowing, and drank the glass of holy water that stood on the table with bull-frogs careering round in it. She shook hands with everybody she knew, and with everybody she didn't know, and kissed the baby. There was no pride about Mrs McDoolan.

The ceremony was about to commence. Joe and the young Todds and the young Taits, who, with the tomahawk and some dogs—about twenty-six dogs—had been up the paddock hunting kangaroo-rats, returned with a live jew-lizard. They squatted round the door guarding the trophy.

Dad and Mother, with the baby in a dress of rebellious hues, stood up and faced the parson. All became silent and expectant. The parson whispered something to Mother, and she placed the baby in Dad's great arms. The band of hunters at the door giggled, and the jew-lizard tried to escape. Dad, his hair and beard grown very long, stared at the parson with a look of wild, weird reverence about him.

"In the name of the Father," the parson drawled, dipping his fingers into the water and letting it drip on to the baby's face, "I baptize thee, Barthol—"

Interruption.

The jew-lizard escaped and, with open mouth and head up, raced across the floor. Had it been a boa-constrictor or a bunyip the women couldn't have squealed with more enthusiasm. It made straight for Judy Jubb. But Judy had been chased by a jew-lizard before. She drew back her skirts, also her leg, and kicked the vermin in the chest and lifted it to the rafters. It fell behind the sofa and settled on Todd's bulldog that was planted there. Bully seized it and shook it vigorously and threw it against Mrs McDoolan, and seized it again and shook it more, shook it until our dog and a pack of others rushed in. "T' the devil!" said Dad indignantly, aiming heavy kicks at the brutes. "The child! Gimme the child!" Mother shrieked, pulling at Dad. "Out w' y'!" said Anderson, letting fly his foot. "Down, Bully!" shouted Todd, and between them all they kicked the dogs right through the door, then heaved the lizard after them.

But the ceremony was soon over, and everybody was radiant with joy, everybody but Bartholomew. He had been asleep until the parson dropped the water on his face, when he woke suddenly. He glared at the strange assemblage a moment, then whined and cried hard. Mother shushed him and danced him up and down, saying, "Did they frigh—ten 'im?" Mrs McDoolan took him and shushed him and jumped him about and said, "There now, there now."

But Bartholomew resented it all and squealed till it seemed that some part of him must burst. Mrs Todd and Mrs Anderson and Judy Jubb each had a go at him. "Must have the wind," murmured Mrs Ryan feelingly, and Mrs Johnson agreed with her by nodding her head. Mother took him again and showed him the dog, but he didn't care for dogs. Then Sal ran out with him and put him on the gee-gee, the parson's old moke that stood buried in thought at the fence, and he was quiet.

A long table erected in the barn was laden with provisions, and Dad invited the company to come along and make a start. They crowded in and stared about. Green boughs and corn-cobs hung on the walls, some bags of shelled corn stood in one corner, and from a beam dangled a set of useless old cart-harness that Dad used to lend anyone wanting to borrow. Dad and Paddy Maloney took up the carving. Dad stood at one end of the table, Paddy at the other. Both brandished long knives. Dad proceeded silently, Paddy with joyous volubility. "Fowl or pig?" he shouted, and rattled the knife, and piled the provender on their plates, and told them to "back in their carts" when they wanted more; and he called the minister "Boss". Paddy was in his element.

It was a magnificent feast and went off most successfully. It went off until only the ruins remained. Then the party returned to the house and danced. Through the afternoon, and far into the night, the concertina screeched its cracked refrain, while the forms of weary females, with muffled infants in their arms, hovered about the drays in the yard, and dog-tired men, soaked to the knees with dew-wet grass, bailing and blocking horses in a paddock corner, took strange, shadowy shape. It wasn't until all was bright and the sun seemed near that the last dray rolled heavily away from the christening of Bartholomew.

Chapter II

SOME TROUBLE WITH A STEER

DEPTH of winter! A cold morning at Shingle Hut. Everything coated with frost. The ground and the woodheap and the water-cask white with it.

The draught-horses stood at the barn, humping their backs, and greedily eating from their nose-bags. The aged saddle-mare, which mostly subsisted on dry grass and long rides, leant over the slip-rails and gazed ponderingly at them. In a corner of the yard a brindle cow, that Dad one day had dehorned with a rail, joyously munched shelled corn-cobs, while near the house an inquisitive steer, with a lumpy jaw, cautiously approached the pig bucket.

Joe, who had brought the horses in, warmed his bare feet at the fire, and sat to breakfast alone, with his hat on. The others had finished and were about. He poured out some tea, and was commencing on a plate of fried pumpkin, left at the fire for him, when Jacko, a half-grown pet kangaroo,

114

bounded hurriedly in at the door. He fouled the table and fell, spreading his ungainly form on the floor, and resting some of his tail calmly on the fire. Then he rose with amusing alacrity and darted into the back room. Joe laughed and ate more pumpkin. A smell of singed marsupial reached him, and he chuckled again. Then he called to Jacko to know what had happened. The kangaroo was dumb. Joe called again. Dad appeared at the door, out of breath, and wet to the hips with dew from the greenstuff. He faced Joe angrily and said, "Where's that damned kangaroo?"

Joe took in the situation instantly and was about to say he didn't know when Jacko sneezed in his own peculiar way and betrayed himself. Dad entered the room and dragged him out.

"Hand me that knife," he demanded with fearful earnestness, reaching towards the table with one hand, while he strained to retain Jacko with the other. Joe hesitated. Again, "Hand me that kni-knife!"

The kangaroo was struggling. Joe was motionless and sullen. Finally Dad secured the weapon himself. Then, "No, no, D-d-dad. Don't!" Joe pleaded. "Don't kill him!" But without another word Dad forced back Jacko's head, till the skin over the throat almost cracked, then drew the knife across it. Joe clutched his arm and squealed, "Murder!" Dad shook him off, and again swished the blade across. Again Joe squealed. Still Jacko struggled. Dad struck him on the snout, and kicked him heavily in the ribs. Joe moaned. Jacko was subdued.

Then Dad proceeded leisurely to use the knife as a saw. But the thing refused to make as much as a mark. Dad got disgusted. He took the marsupial in his arms and heaved it out of the door on top of the dog, which was staring in at Joe's breakfast. The dog yelped, and limped away, but the kangaroo bounced up like a football and attempted to re-enter. Dad's large, heavy boot met him at the door. It caught him full in the stomach, and lifted him back again. Jacko wisely disappeared round the house.

Dad turned to Joe. Joe moved to the other end of the table.

"You blockhead!" Dad commenced, moving nearer him. "Didn't I tell you to get rid of that damned thing?" A pause. "Didn't I?"

Joe made no answer, but prepared for action. He placed both hands on the table, and, crouching in a springing attitude, eyed his parent in an interested way.

"Didn't I tell you to keep it off the greenstuff?" No reply. Dad edged round the table. So did Joe. Then Dad sprang at him and secured a piece of his shirt-sleeve. Joe grinned involuntarily.

"Stand!" cried Dad, reversing his course, Joe doing likewise. "Stir another inch, and I'll knock your brains out!" He brandished the teapot.

Joe stirred fully a foot.

"Stand," Dad repeated, "or by—!" But Joe didn't stand. He dodged one way, then another, and, kicking down a stool that was in his way, bounded across the room and out the door. The teapot followed him.

A few moments later Dad was harnessing the plough-horses, while Joe, with tears in his eyes, sat concealed behind the haystack. He was despondent and remained quiet for a while, thinking and chewing straw. He noticed Dave a short distance away, digging potatoes and putting them into a bucket. He wished to speak to Dave confidentially. He felt a desire to make Dave unhappy. He would tell him that he was going to clear out, and leave Dad and the selection and the pet kangaroo and everything else to go to glory. He would break up the happy home.

Dave wasn't far off, but Joe deemed it unsafe to whistle or call to him, for fear of betraying his whereabouts to Dad.

He stood up and waved his hat about to attract Dave's attention. Dave worked on. Joe paused to think. Then he gave a grotesque exhibition of high jumping. Dave dropped more potatoes into the bucket. Joe reflected again, and an idea occurred to him. With one eye round the corner of the stack in the direction of Dad, he crept out and secured a stone. He was an excellent shot, or believed he was, and thought to lodge the missile in the bucket, to attract Dave.

Gathering himself together, he let fly. The stone landed with a thud on the broad of Dave's back, and raised dust from his shirt. Gods, how he jumped and dropped the spade! He contorted his features, screwed and twisted about, and looked up and down. His attention was attracted.

Joe stood still, alarmed and unable to decide what to do. At last Dave's eyes rested on him.

There was an enraged howl, and, with the spade uplifted,

117

Dave ran towards him. Joe decided on action. He fled. Making straight for the back door of the house, he surprised the lumpy jawed steer poking among the pots, his head buried to the horns in a kerosene tin. The startled beast sprang back, and the tin went with him. He had pressed his head into it till it became a tight fit. He looked foolish, and twirled round and round with it. It clung to him. He paused and pondered. Gradually his tail rose to a horizontal position. Then, without warning, he bellowed and blindly stampeded across the yard. The brindle cow started up inquiringly, and some cattle of Anderson's came running down the lane. He carried a portion of an old bark shed away, and nearly brought down Dave, who was hurrying in pursuit of Joe. Dave heaved the spade at the brute, and called to Dad to look out.

Dad glanced round and saw the steer coming. "Way! Way!" he cried to one of the horses (Captain, a newly broken colt) as he was throwing a back-hand across the other. But Captain was nervous. He snorted and turned his head just in time to see the steer collide with the dray. That was enough. Before Dad could reach him he made off, careering madly round and round the yard. The steer wasn't in it with him, particularly when his legs became entangled in the chains. Dave said he never saw prettier bucking. He bucked until there wasn't a stitch of harness left on him, then he fell over the fence into the cultivation and galloped away lame.

Dad didn't speak. He stood watching Captain, until a low, pathetic bellow broke the silence. He turned and saw the steer. The brute was on the broad of its back, between the shafts of the dray, its legs beating the air. Dad went to it and feelingly kicked the tin off its nose. Then he took a rail and poked till it struggled to its feet and departed.

That night, after supper, as Dad and Dave and Joe cleaned the guns and cheerfully talked of going out possum shooting, and as the smaller ones played and prattled merrily on the bag carpet before the glowing fire, no one would have suspected that the harmony of our household had ever been disturbed.

Chapter III

GOOD-BYE TO THE OLD HOME

"KIT! Kit!" called Sarah, standing at the back door with a saucer of milk. The kitten lay in the sun, blinked at her, and rolled over playfully, but didn't come. "You're too well fed!" said Sarah, retreating into the kitchen. The kitten purred lazily to signify that that was so.

Everything was well fed at Shingle Hut now. A change had come. An air of prosperity was about the place. Broad-backed, upstanding draught-horses, fat and fresh, fed around contentedly; the paddock was stocked with sleek, well-bred cows and spring heifers, and four and five-year-old bullocks fit for a show; the reaper and binder in the shed was all our own, two ploughs were going, and—ye money-lenders!— the mortgage had been paid right off.

For six successive years our wheat crop had been a big success. No matter what Dad did he couldn't go wrong. Whenever he was compelled to sow late there was sure to be too much rain and early crops would run rank, or take the rust or the smut or something, while ours would come on nicely and be a success. Or else no rain at all would fall—somehow it would wait for Dad—and when Anderson's and Johnson's and all the wheat about was parched and perished, ours was a picture good to see. And Dad earned and enjoyed a reputation for long-headedness, for persistence and practical farming. People praised him and pointed to him as a pattern for their sons to follow—an example of what could be accomplished on the land by industry and a bit of brains.

Yet Dad wasn't satisfied. He talked of selling out, of taking up a thousand acres somewhere and expanding operations. But Mother opposed it; she thought we were doing well enough. Shingle Hut was good enough for her. She had worked hard and spent the best of her days in it, scraping and struggling, and all she asked now was to live the rest of her life there—to die peacefully and be buried near the house.

The rest of us agreed with Dad. We wanted a change. What the result might be we didn't consider—we only wished to shift. Ripping up the old house, rounding up the stock, camping under a dray a night or two on the way to the Promised Land, gave food for delightful speculation. We longed for it all to come about.

"See anything of him?" Dad asked, as Dave rode into the yard and dismounted, after searching for a lost horse one day.

"No," Dave said, and leant on the fence and nibbled the end of a straw. Dad leant on the other side and reflected.

A short distance off a new building was going up. Donald McIntyre, a broad-shouldered Scotsman with a passion for politics, and one McDonald, who didn't believe in governments at all, and confined his studies solely to the weather and pumpkins and profanity, were building a humpy with a shingling hammer. Donald McIntyre was on the rafters, arguing wildly and shaking the hammer menacingly at

McDonald, who was on the ground.

Dad and Dave looked up.

"Come doon, ye —— ——!" shouted McDonald, and McIntyre sprang from the rafters and pursued him round and round the humpy.

"A fight!" Dave said excitedly. "Come on!" And he ran a few paces. But at the same moment Joe rushed to the scene out of breath.

"I fuf-fuf-found 'im, Dad!" he said excitedly.

"Where?" Dad asked eagerly.

"Bub-bub-bet y' can't gug-guess?"

"Where the devil is he, boy?"

("Look at McIntyre, after him across the ploughed ground!"—enthusiastically from Dave.)

"Down the w-w-well!"

"What?" Dad hissed, showing his teeth and punching the wind with his fist.

"Is he dead?" he added.

"Don't know th-that, Dad, but he s-s-smells!"

Dad groaned and walked inside and out again, then round the yard.

"Yoke up Gypsy and Tiger," he said sternly to Dave, "and bring them down." Then he went off to the well by himself.

Dad peered into the well a moment and drew back and pulled a very ugly face.

Dave arrived with the horses. He went to the well to look down but ran away and spat.

Joe held the horses and chuckled.

Dave thought of the wind. It was blowing towards him. He made a wide circuit and approached the well on the other side. But when he leant forward to look down, the wind changed and he ran away again. Dad was determined. He advanced with a frown and a heavy rope, fastened one end of the latter to a sapling close by, and hurled the rest of it into the well. Then he, too, retreated.

"Now," he said to Dave, "go down and fasten it on 'im!"

"Me?" Dave said, backing farther away.

Joe chuckled again.

"Well, y' don't expect me to go down, do y'?" Dad snorted.

Dave grinned a sickly grin.

"It won't kill y', will it?" Then, after a pause, "Are y' going t' do it—or not?" There were shell and shrapnel in Dad's eye, and he looked ugly.

"W-w-wet y'r nose, Dave," Joe said, advisedly.

Dave hesitated, then reluctantly descended. He disappeared along the rope and was below some time. He came to the surface again, and gasped and staggered and threw himself on the grass and seemed ill. Change of air didn't do Dave much good.

Dad fastened the horses to the rope and told them to get up. The chains jerked and tightened. Gypsy and Tiger hung in their collars and strained, and tore the ground with their toes. Dad shouted and waved a big stick over them. Captain's form gradually rose till his head was in sight and his nose caught against the sleepers that lined the mouth of the well. Then he stopped.

"Gypsy . . . Tiger!" Dad roared, and rattled the stick encouragingly on their hides. Gypsy and Tiger began to tire, and eased off.

"Look out!" Dave cried. "Don't let them back!" Dad seized their heads and held on. But the dead horse gradually descended again, and was slowly dragging the live ones and Dad after it. Dad struck Gypsy on the nose with his fist to make her stand up. Gypsy reared and fell across the well and kicked desperately. Then Tiger tried to turn round in his chains and lost his footing and lay on his back, his tail hanging down the well. Dad was horror-stricken. He threw away his hat and ran in several directions in search of something. He found a sapling, lifted it, threw it down again, and ran back to the horses and held his hands above his head like a preacher.

Sal came to tell Dad he was wanted at the house, but he couldn't hear her.

"Curse it, can't y' do something?" he cried to Dave.

Then Gypsy made a big effort to rise and fell down the well and dragged Tiger's harness with her. Tiger jumped up and made off. Dad stared aghast.

"W-w-what did y' hit 'er f'?" Joe asked reproachfully.

"Yah!" Dad bellowed, and sprang at Joe. Joe didn't look behind till he reached the house.

But Burton happened to come along with his bullock team, and rescued Gypsy and dragged Captain's corpse from the well. Then Dad went for a drink of water in the gully and sat down under a bush, and Sal came and spoke to him again, and when he was calm he went to the house.

The man from town who had offered us four hundred pounds for the selection was at the house waiting. They went inside.

"Well," said the visitor, "have you considered my offer?"

"Yes," Dad answered, "I'll take it!"—and Shingle Hut was sold!

Mother clutched her knees with both hands and stared hard and silently at the fireplace till her eyes filled with tears. Sal ran out to Dave and Joe, and the three of them discussed the turn things had taken. Mother came out to them.

"It's sold?" Sal said.

"Yes," Mother replied slowly, "it's s-s-sold." And again the tears came, and she sat on a sleeper beside the barn and, hiding her face in her apron, cried hard.

Sal hung her head and thought, but Dave went to Mother

and sat beside her, and tried to explain the advantages of selling out and beginning afresh. The man left the house, walked to his horse, shook hands with Dad, and went away.

Then Dad paced up and down, up and down, and round about by himself for a long, long time.

A cold, dull day. Heavy black clouds hung low and darkened the earth. At intervals a few drops of rain fell, a deluge threatened. No gentle winds blew, no birds whistled among the boughs. Dave was passing slowly out at the slip-rails with a dray-load of furniture and farm implements, Joe sitting astride Dad's old saddle-mare, in charge of the cows in the lane, Dad loading a second dray, Sal putting a horse in the spring-cart, the rest of us gathering knick-knacks and things about the place. We were leaving, leaving Shingle Hut, the old house we had known so long, the old home where Kate was married, where Bill and Tom and Barty were born, the home where merriment so often mocked misfortune and light hearts and hope softened the harshness of adversity.

And Anderson and Mrs Anderson came to see us off—kind-hearted people were the Andersons. And Judy Jubb came all the way from Prosperity Peak to kiss Sal.

"Good-bye, then, and God bless y'," Mrs Anderson said, her large eyes swimming in tears. Mother held out her hand, but broke down and was helped into the spring-cart.

" 'N' I hope y' won't regret it," Anderson said as he shook Dad's hand. Then with a last look around—a look of lingering affection—we bade farewell to Shingle Hut and started for Our New Selection.

Chapter IV

A FRESH START

THUS we came to Saddletop. Dad looking old, Mother older, Sarah tall and womanly, Dave a big, bony man, more reserved than ever, Joe approaching manhood, broad-shouldered, sturdy, full-faced and droll—he was our own comedian, entertained us often, and gave us pains in the side by taking people off. The younger ones all stretching out, and—no more babies.

Our new selection was a piece of magnificent country, twelve hundred acres, all rich black soil ten to fifteen feet deep, permanent water, and a government well outside the fence; a wide fringe of heavy timber at the back; plain in front, and grass!—we used to lose the horses in it.

The house was new, a stately palace, after Shingle Hut; five rooms in it; weather-boarded, floor-boarded, iron-roofed; lock and key to every door; kitchen, and a thousand-gallon tank. And such water! We had never known the taste of real water before. No charcoal, no ashes, no traces of a drought, no doubtful flavour of any kind about it, and no scum to scrape off whenever we boiled some.

And Dad was proud of the selection. He was pleased with our prospects altogether, and talked of the progress the district was making.

Saddletop was a rising place. A branch railway line was coming to it—had been coming for twenty-two years. Farmers from South Australia were there—men who, 'twas said, knew how to farm, who understood all about soils and silos, and worked on scientific principles. They were settled along a deserted gully where nothing but burr and thistle and nut-grass grew, and whenever it rained hard they would retreat in disorder to high land, with their wives in barrows and their beds and things on their backs.

There was one farmer from Victoria. He knew something about selecting. He came and rooted the trees out of his land and put in wheat, and watched it grow for a while, then went away one morning and never came back.

A number of old pioneers were there, just beginning to do well after thirty years of toil and struggle, their difficulties and dangers and innumerable hardships but faintly compre-hended.

Up dry gullies and blind gullies, hidden away behind ranges and rocks, were selectors who hoed holes in the long grass and dropped pumpkin seed into them, then went away somewhere and came back with a horse at the end of a long rope, which they handled and broke for somebody while the pumpkin was growing.

There were a few of a species who, in wet weather, stood all day long in their doorway with a wet bag on their shoulders, gazing out philosophically on the pelting rain, and when it wasn't raining, went away with a blanket and looked for shearing.

A weird, silent "hatter" was there, whose hair penetrated his hat, and who stitched patches on his pants with a packing needle and string—the strange man who lived under the range away from everybody, in a bark hut propped up on the downhill side by a stick; the man who avoided all human society; whose hut contained harness, flung on the floor, and scraps of greenhide, and a greasy table with sapling legs driven into the ground; who sat anywhere on the floor, and took his dinner off a tin plate placed on his knees, and asked questions of his watchful dog, and told it things while the birds of the bush came round the open door and hopped in and out unmolested; the man who never grumbled, whose happiness was the silence and solitude of his surroundings, whose God was Nature and whose only hell the toothache.

The selector of regular movements was there—the methodical man who caught the same old horse each morning by gladdening the steed's heart with the sound of the same few handfuls of corn rattled in a dish, and who always went somewhere. His form was known in the district miles off. He was a clock to those working in the fields. They told the time of day by him as he passed along.

There were people from the town there, too—broken-down swells who professed hatred for the bush and were always going back to the city, but never started; polite people who wouldn't drink tea out of a saucer, who loved flower-gardens (and grew one geranium in a tin), whose daughters declared all the young men around rough because they neglected to lift their hats, and who came out in holland riding habits because they were cheap, and said they were all the fashion in town.

There was one man who regularly employed men, who possessed everything necessary about a farm and stored his hay in sheds, and drew cheques. He was the squire of the district He always travelled to town by train, first class, and never said good day to the neighbours, except in moments of absent-mindedness. He might have been worth a thousand pounds. People often called him a millionaire and it never worried him; it made him less absent-minded. He met ministerial parties and influential visitors to the district at the railway station and drove them in a buggy to his house, and entertained them, and showed them over the farm, and filled the "special correspondent" with inspirations of his (the squire's) own enterprise, and ideas about "prosperous selectors", and "a district with a future".

Scattered about in remote places were average selectors, the plodders—men who poked along leisurely and reared large families and took reverses as cheerfully as they took pills; men who placed large stones and heavy fencing material on the roof to keep it from flying off when there was any wind (the roof kept the stones from falling through and shattering the dinner table when there was no wind); men who reckoned they could make money and save, if only the seasons could be relied on and they had no interest to meet.

And, some distance from each other, a small school, surrounded by gum-trees, and two unpainted churches of battered, warlike appearance, raised their heads. The school children battered them. They frequently quarrelled over religion on the way from school, and, since there was no one to read the Riot Act to them, wrecked each other's church with stones.

We had not been long at Saddletop when we became acquainted with these people. Many of them came to welcome us to the district—some to borrow things.

Miss Wilkins and Miss Mulrooney were among the first to come. They came one bright afternoon when the air was fresh and the sky was blue, when the birds were singing and the butterflies fluttering, when Dad and Cranky Jack were trenching for fruit-trees and Dave and Joe ploughing on the plain.

They slid off their horses at the fence surrounding the house and laughed. The laugh was to attract attention. They stepped onto the veranda and curtseyed and said it was a lovely day. Mother invited them in. They hesitated as though time were precious, and Miss Wilkins said, "We can only stay just a minute, Mrs Rudd." Then they sat down and poked out the toes of their boots from under their habits, and looked through the corners of their eyes at everything in the room, and didn't go away till dusk.

Miss Wilkins was a stout person, fat and flabby, and owned to being five-and-twenty. She had owned to five-and-twenty for sixteen years. She laced tight, too, and fancied herself thin and shapely. Polly Palethorpe and Annie Hayes (both jammed into one wouldn't equal her size) were objects of astonishment to her.

Miss Mulrooney had a figure and was only twenty-eight. She had seen some town life, too, and was one of those who wore a holland habit. There were hints of vanished finery about her. She was hard up, in fact, and strove to conceal her poverty by putting on airs.

She sat and drank tea and ate scones and fresh butter with much gusto, praised the provender every time she reached for more, and asked Mother if she made the scones herself— as if she would call in a traveller or get Dad to bake them!

Miss Wilkins talked to Sal about a dance that was at the Rise, and Jim Murphy courting Norah Fahey, and old Fahey chasing Jim with a gun, punctuating her conversation with loud cheerful shrieks. And Miss Mulrooney told Mother in tired tones how hard it was on them all to have to rough it in the bush after being so well off in town, used to their carriage and servants. (Her father, the story went, had been employed by a lawyer in Brisbane as confidential clerk. He used to open the "private" door whenever a client came, which was nearly once a month, and inquire in a respectful tone of the empty chair if he were engaged; then he would hand the client another chair without making a noise and steal out into the street to find the lawyer and drag him in by a back way.) She assured Mother (and Mother, good soul, believed her and felt deeply for the family) that she didn't know how they would live at all only for the little money papa was still receiving from the business in town, as there was nothing at all to be got out of farming.

And as they talked and drank more tea the schoolmaster's wife and Mary O'Reilly and Miss Perkins approached the house. Miss Wilkins saw them through the window and whispered to Miss Mulrooney. Miss Mulrooney fidgeted and was uneasy, but, recognizing the horses fastened to the fence, the schoolmaster's wife and Mary O'Reilly and Miss Perkins turned their heads away and rode past. They weren't speaking to Miss Wilkins or Miss Mulrooney.

Gray (the squire of the district) came one morning. He merely looked in because he happened to be passing. But he wouldn't come inside—that would be making himself cheap. He stayed in the yard and talked with an air of superior knowledge to Dad.

"What do you want with a thing like that?" he said, pointing to a new three-furrow plough. (He was a stale conservative who wouldn't see, and regarded everything new with contempt.)

"To plough with, and save time and labour," Dad answered.

"Save your grandmother!" Gray said. "I've a couple of single-furrows over there," he went on, indicating his farm, "and I guarantee any of my men'll turn over as much land in a day with any one of them as you will with that."

"Well," said Dad, "send a man along with one, an' we'll see."

"And plough your land for you?" Gray went away.

And Sam Evans came, and stood on the veranda, bashfully turning an old hat round and round in his hands, and wouldn't step inside because the place was clean. But Barney Ballantyne would. He said 'it was "cheaper sittin' than standin' '", and he sat down on Sarah's hat that had been left on a chair, and told Dad lies about wheat crops, and chewed tobacco, and spat squares and circles till they evolved into carpet patterns on the cleanly scrubbed floor.

Many others called and in due course we returned their visits. We mixed with them in their homes, mingled with them abroad, shared their successes, their prejudices and sympathies, joined with them in song and sorrow in these new surroundings, and among new friends and true friends we faced the vagaries of fortune afresh and commenced a new life.

Chapter V

THE GREAT MILK ENTERPRISE

A T first we encountered reverses. No rain for months;
nothing but heat—heat and scorching gales. Then it
rained when we least required it, in the middle of the
hay-making, and poured for weeks—poured till the cut-off
thirty acres of oats, the only crop in the district, rotted and
was ruined.

Two successive seasons the wheat failed. Once, when it
had grown higher than the fence, a late frost blackened and
withered it all up in one night, and once it didn't grow at all.

"Don't know," said Dad gloomily, "don't know at all."
Then, after reflecting, "Jimmy Tyson himself couldn't
stand much o' these seasons. Most uncertain. A season or two
more, 'n' a man might lose all he's ever earned an' not have a
bloomin' stick."

Dad's reflections only made him unhappy. He wasn't as
brave as he used to be, and the loss of a few pounds worried
him and gave him nightmares. Dad was fond of money now.
He thought more of it than he did of Mother.

Dad complained of his prospects to old Martin McEvoy
of the Twelve Mile. Martin believed in butter. He milked a
few old cows and once or twice a week trotted his cart to
the railway station; and the inhabitants of Saddletop would
stand at their doors and stare and grin at him whenever he
passed along the road. Martin and his butter were sources
of amusement to them. They regarded it as undignified to
take round a lot of old milkers and drag fluid out of them.
They were farmers.

133

L

"I can't see what you've t' growl about," McEvoy said, casting an eye over our lucerne-paddocks and at the cattle camped near the gate. "If I hed them paddocks and them cows I'd mek a thousan' a year."

Dad grunted his incredulity.

"I would—no darn mistake." A pause. "Out o' ten I mek four quid a week now!" And Martin looked defiant.

"Out o' butter?" Dad stared.

"Yes, butter!" Martin shouted. "A long sight better'n wheat." Then he jumped from his cart and dragged some papers from his greasy trouser-pocket. He showed Dad an invoice and a cheque. Dad didn't take his eyes off the cheque till Martin returned it to his pocket with a triumphant snort; then he looked at the lucerne-paddocks and the cows and thought. Martin drove on.

For several days Dad was inactive. He spent his time in a chair on the veranda. Dave and Joe missed him in the paddock. They wished he would stay on the veranda all his life. But Dad was only working out a problem.

Dad left the veranda suddenly one afternoon and went among the cattle. A fine-looking lot they were—sleek and fat—but beyond an odd one killed for our own use, which mostly went bad in the cask and was thrown out, they were only a nuisance on the place and devoured more hay than they were worth. To Dad, though, they were priceless. He was never done with admiring them. They were his pictures, his oil paintings, his art gallery.

"Sixty-five cows . . . twenty-six pounds a week," Dad muttered and returned to the house and sat till tea. Dad was cheerful and questioned Dave about the ploughing. Then he broke new ground and spoke enthusiastically of dairying. He went into figures and said the cow-yard was to be put in working order the next day. Dave was silent. Sarah was inclined to debate the matter, but Dad silenced her. "I've

thought it all out," he said, waving his hand, "and know just what I'm about."

Breaking day. A hard, biting frost that whitened everything and crunched and cracked beneath you when you walked was over the land. Cold! Charity was nothing to it. The horses stood shivering at the big gate, waiting for their hay, cockatoos screamed in the trees up the gully, Cook's roosters crowed faintly in the distance—ours lustily answered back—horse bells tinkled-tankled on the reserve, the smoke of a camp-fire curled into the frosty air, forms of horsemen moved quietly about and a thousand head of travelling cattle took shape.

A whip crack, a shout or two, and the cows, with Bill close on their heels, rushed into the yard.

Dave and Joe and Cranky Jack came out, grumbled at the cold, stared at the travelling cattle moving from the reserve, and started milking. They milked in silence and were nearly finished when Dad's angry voice was heard at the barn. He wanted to know why the devil the horses were not fed, and shuffled about yelling for Bill.

Sarah brought a can of hot tea and some bread and butter into the yard. Dad came along swinging his arms.

"They don't want that here," he snapped. "Take it away!"

Joe grabbed some of the provender and swilled a cup of tea. Sarah grinned.

Dad scowled and measured the milk in the tins with his eye, then entered the yard and inspected the cows and stared sternly at the milkmen. Dad was a watchful overseer.

Dad turned and called boisterously to Sarah as she returned to the house. Joe, in a cheerful mood, pointed a cow's teat over his shoulder and directed a stream of milk at Dad. Dad danced round and looked in the air and down at his feet and wiped his neck with his hand. Then he growled at a red cow that was facing him, shaking her head and throwing froth from her nose.

Joe entered into an argument, across the yard, with Dave about a pony mare of Doolan's.

"Get on with the milkin'," Dad said impatiently, "an' let the cows out—lots to be done without yarnin'." And he hobbled round again, returning to the same spot and exhibiting increased impatience.

"She's by B-b-badger," Joe went on.

"Gerrout!" Dave said.

"B-b-bet y' quid." And, as if to book the bet, Joe stood up, placing his bucket on the ground.

"Dammit!" Dad hollered. "Why 'n the devil can't y' get on? Are y' goin' to be—?"

Joe looked at him. The red cow with the frothy nose had approached Dad closely, and seemed to mistake him for a heap of hay. She wasn't a handsome beast however you viewed her, or a dangerous-looking one, either.

"L--l-look out that red cow d-d-don't charge," Joe said (which was the last thing in the world he expected the brute to do).

Dad glanced down quickly. He was taken by surprise. Sudden consciousness of the cow's proximity startled him. Like a rooster hit with a brick when half-way up his top note, he cut short a yell intended for Joe and lifting his big right foot aimed a heavy kick at the cow's head. His boot, a hard, ill-shaped blucher, grazed her forehead and, sliding under the animal's hoop horns, held fast. The cow swung round. Dad dropped on his back, clutched with both hands at the ground, and waved his left leg menacingly at the brute. Finding Dad a fixture, she became hysterical. She bellowed and ran backwards and put her tongue out in an ugly curl.

"My G-G-God! Help, help!" Dad shouted. The other

cows rushed round the yard. One shoved the rails down, and they all passed out.

Dave and Joe sprang to Dad's assistance. Neither, for the moment, could see a way to extricate him. Cranky Jack jammed a finger into each of his ears and laughed, and looked humorous. Dave rushed to the cow's horns, Joe to her tail, then the other way about.

Round the yard the cow backed, bellowing more and more. She trampled over Joe's bucket and spilt the milk, and wiped it up with Dad.

Joe at last seized Dad's hands and pulled back, pulled till he lost footing and fell down. Then the cow backed right out of the yard, bumping Dad heavily on the fallen rails. Dad cursed at every bump. She proceeded backwards towards the barn. Sarah rushed on the scene, wailing, "Oh, my gracious!" —and frightened the beast more. Joe recovered himself and seized Dad's hands again. Two small dogs, constant companions of Dad's, arrived. They barked and bit the air near the cow's head, sometimes near Dad's, and fell over one another in a struggle for position, till at last Dave, who got tired of shouting to them, let go Dad's leg, which he was struggling to release, and kicked one of them into the air.

Mother, in state of wild alarm, appeared and added to the uselessness of Dad's rescuers. Dad lost his hat; he was covered with dust and his shirt came out and hung over his head like a bag. He looked very undignified.

The cow went back against the dog kennel. A bull-dog was tied there. He crouched down and waited for her. "Give us a pull 'ere—quick," Dave gasped, and Joe jumped to his side. "Little more, now sh—" Just then the dog fastened his teeth in the cow's leg. She roared and plunged forward, knocked Dave and Joe down and trampled all over Dad. Then she dishonestly raced out of the gate with only Dad's boot under her horn.

The Great Milk Enterprise

We picked Dad up and dusted him and set him on the veranda to cool. Mother gave him a cup of hot tea. She said he looked as if he needed it. He said he felt as if he did.

Somehow, after that day, Dad took no interest in the milk enterprise. He found other jobs for us, and Cranky Jack forgot to bring the cows in and was not reprimanded.

In a week or so we had forgotten Dad's dream of fortune and were once more busy with hard graft. And presently Dad said that he believed things were on the mend.

Chapter VI

DAD IN DISTRESS

How time passes! Those days of toil and moil, that weary, uphill struggle at Shingle Hut, were now thought of only in moments of merriment. Queer old days, wild old ways that all of us loved to remember, none of us wished to forget.

Farming was not the drag, the wretched, murderous drudgery, it used to be. We were improving every day, climbing rapidly to the lap of comfort. The wheat turned out a success again, and the profit made us all rejoice. Still we kept our heads. The frequent want of a shilling had taught us the worth of one. We were not extravagant. Mother, in her thankfulness, attributed our success to the mercy and goodness of God. Dad reckoned it was all due to his own head.

"Well, yes," he would sometimes admit, on being pressed, "the boys do a good deal, an' the women've done a bit one way or another, too, but all with the hands; an' where'd be the good of it if there were no head? Their hands, but my head!"

On that point Dad was emphatic. From his decision there was no appeal. Dad was the Judge, the Full Court, and the Privy Council, too, on our selection.

Things were worked methodically, almost reduced to a science. To Dave was allotted a three-furrow plough and a set of horses which none but himself used; Joe had a double-furrow and separate horses; Little Bill rose at cockcrow and brought all horses from the grass-paddock and drove them back last thing at night—drove them gently in obedience to Dad's orders until he got out of sight, when he rushed and raced them for their lives and flogged them through the rails. The horses did their best to get through without maiming themselves, but the odds were always on Little Bill.

Dad poked and pottered about, didn't do much, in fact did very little in a most impressive way. He fed the horses, and patched bags, and made a leg-rope occasionally, and sooled the dog on the fowls if ever they approached the cultivation, and cooeed and shook his fist menacingly at Dave and Joe when they sat on the ploughs yarning, and followed in the tracks of the men who pulled and gathered the corn, and found cobs they missed, and swore. He rarely remained longer than a minute in one place; he was every-where, warning and worrying everyone. He praised the farm and explained things to anyone who called and in a lofty manner disregarded the solicitations of travellers. He put them all off with an eloquent wave of the hand. Travellers were not fond of Dad.

A bright, sunny day, after a heavy frost. Dave and Joe following the ploughs, up and down, and round and round.

Joe came to a standstill and stared across the field.

"What the deuce is he after now?" he said, following the running form of Dad with his eyes.

Dave stopped his team and stared also.

Dad crossed the cultivation, entered the grass-paddock, and ran along a wide gully through some thick timber. Three of the Regan boys, from fourteen to twenty years old, were there doing something with a stout, springy sapling. They had it bent, bow-fashion, to the ground, and kept in position by a lever. A wire noose was fastened to the sapling. It was an ingenious arrangement they had conceived to catch dingoes with, and they were standing contemplating its construction. Dad came with a rush, and tried to fall on one of them. But the Regans were all runners. They decamped.

"If I don't make y'r eyes black when I catch y'r, then damn me!" Dad shouted after them. They ran harder.

Dad turned to the bent sapling, looked at it, wondered what it meant. He kicked up leaves and dirt in search of enlightenment. He kicked his foot into the noose and tripped. The sapling left the lever and flew up, taking Dad with it. Dad was enlightened. The sapling wasn't strong enough to swing all of him in the air; it elevated his heels till only his head and chest and arms were in touch with the ground. He swung like a slaughtered bullock partly hoisted to the gallows. He swore lamentably, he roared and wriggled, he kicked with the limb that was free, and clutched at the grass. He bared a patch of ground about his head and went through a series of swimming movements with his hands. Yet he swung.

A pocket-knife and a two-shilling piece fell out of his trouser-pocket. He clutched them and held them fast in his hand. Then he ceased struggling and began to use his head.

Dave and Joe were still staring in the direction of the gully and wondering. But they were nearly a mile off.

Regan's dog, which had gone hunting through the paddock on its own account while the Regan boys were setting
the snare, returned panting to the place. It was a dog with
a lot of the bull breed in it, an ugly, surly, sulky dog with a
thick drooping under-lip. It had a bad name in the district.
Dad knew of its reputation. It trotted up. Dad was hanging
motionless, thinking.

He heard the noise. Feelings of hope and thankfulness
entered his soul. He strained, and leaning on his hands turned
his eyes up to welcome his deliverer. He saw the dog and
recognized it and groaned. The dog saw him and stood,
staring. It was surprised, astonished. It growled coarsely,
gruffly. A cold, creepy feeling passed all through Dad. He
glared at the brute with eyes of terror. Then, spurred by
desperation, he kicked vigorously and howled for help. The
dog sprang back, inclined to fly, but seeing that Dad
remained stationary it faced him and barked. And such a
bark!

Dad blackened in the face, his eyes threatened to burst.
He tried to throw the two-shilling piece hard at the dog. It
rolled short. He opened the pocket-knife with his teeth. The
dog came closer. It trotted round Dad, drew still nearer,
barking, barking. Dad flinched and grasped the knife tighter.
There was a pause, on the dog's part. Dad collected his
thoughts. He became resourceful. He softened his voice and
said affectionately, "My poor chap! Poor old fellow! Poor
—old—boy!"

But Regan's dog knew a thing or two; besides, it had
become conscious of Dad's helplessness.

Meanwhile, Dave and Joe, weary of wondering, went
on ploughing. But the Regan boys, attracted by the barking
of their dog, cautiously re-entered the paddock and approached the gully. When in sight of the snare they took

in the situation and ran up, shouting to the dog to desist. The sound of their voices only emboldened the brute. It misunderstood. Their shrieks it took for words of encouragement, and, laying bare its teeth, it rushed in and barked close against Dad's ribs. Dad shuddered and writhed. His flesh twitched. He missed the dog's nose with the pocket-knife. In return the dog snatched a mouthful of his pants and some of his thigh and would have had more only the Regan boys came up and beat it off with sticks.

They released Dad in a hurry and ran away again, and didn't wait for anything. There was nothing mean or mercenary about them.

Dad always referred to that experience as one of the things that had aged him before his time.

Chapter VII

A SURPRISE PARTY

W E saw that changed circumstances had made a new
girl of Sarah. She had an abundance of leisure time
now and revelled in reading the *Family Herald*
and other intellectual papers; took a keen interest in fashions;
studied etiquette hard, and wherever she visited took stock
and learnt things. Norah, teaching in town, supplied her
with much up-to-date information.

Sarah was never done with inflicting new ideas upon us.
She would doll Mother up and parade her round in things
that made the good old soul blush the whole time she was
in them. And such innovations! She scrawled "Ruddville"
on some tin and nailed it to the front gate. She wrote out
laboriously a lot of rules for good manners and tacked up
the list in our room as a kind of perpetual warning. She
checked Dad for stirring his tea with a knife and quarrelled
with Joe if he swigged milk from a jug or grabbed up the
bread and pitched it to her when she asked him nicely to pass
the plate.

The table, too, was never twice laid the same way, while
pieces of furniture constantly swapped corners. Enter the
rooms in the dark and approach the corner where, in the
morning, you had seen the couch, and the chances were you
would wreck the whatnot or tramp on a toy dog or something. Had Sarah been able to slew the house round, she
would have made it face the east one day and the back yard
the next.

One New Year's Eve we had visitors. Farrell's wife was at our place (Farrell, who was the schoolmaster, frequently handed her over to us while he went to town to enjoy himself). Miss Mason, a young lady from town, was spending the week with Sarah. And the Rev. Peter Macfarlane dropped in—but only for dinner.

Sarah called Joe and Bill into the kitchen.

"Have some manners today," she said to Joe, "and don't act as though you had never seen anyone before. And you—" to Bill—"you great gawk, be careful and don't make a fool of yourself."

"We'll be most p-p'-lite," Joe said (he only stuttered occasionally now and often carried pebbles in his mouth to cure himself). And Joe bowed low to the kitchen wall, and inquired how it did and whether it would oblige by "p-p-passing the s-s-spuds". But Bill blushed to the ears. He anticipated a bad time. Like Dave, Bill abhorred company. Dave was sullen over the matter. Bill was fidgety and flurried, and his large, lake-like eyes would roll in their watery sockets.

We were restless. Dinner was very late, but when we were called we forgave Sarah everything, for the table was most inviting. It would have attracted a painter, or a pig, or even a cockatoo, there was so much variety. Ferns, flowers, corn-cobs, wattle blossoms, corn-stalks and things waved all over it, and a large, healthy piece of pumpkin vine sheltered the butter. Sarah stood by, smiling, her hands clasped on her apron, waiting the effect.

Joe was the first to enter. He stood, stared, guffawed rudely, and would have run back only the others were on his heels. "Dear me, girl," said Dad, "what's all this?"

Sarah smiled. Everyone sat down. The visitors talked cheerfully and in turn admired the piece of pumpkin vine.

Dave was solemn and silent and indifferent as a tombstone.

146

Dave had no taste, no eye for art. Joe passed him a corn-cob, and he grinned in his weird way, but, recollecting there was company, composed himself and was silent again. Dave was never boisterous long at a time. He looked along his nose and waited.

Dad rattled a knife on the steel and began to carve.

A short interval of silence.

Mrs Farrell looked at Dave and asked him had he seen the lovely corn Mullins had. As if she couldn't have asked someone else! Dave started, fumbled his fingers, lifted his eyes and dropped them again, but couldn't think of a word to say. Joe rescued him. Joe had seen Mullins's corn.

Dave was very unhappy. He thought everybody must be staring at him, and sat in dread of Mrs Farrell's asking more questions.

"A very, very small helping of fowl, if you please," the parson said, in answer to Dad.

Bill's eyes and mouth moved rapidly. He seemed to be repeating poetry or a prayer to himself.

" 'N' what for you, Bill?"

"Er—a very, very small helping of fowl, if you please," he said rapidly.

Joe made an ugly spluttering noise in his throat which disconcerted Bill. He changed colour.

Sarah tried to frown at Bill, but his eyes were on the parson. Mrs Farrell smiled.

The parson stirred his tea, took up his knife and fork, and began. Bill did these things, too.

Dave was getting on well. The others talked about music and concerts.

"Do you sing, Mr Rudd?" Miss Mason asked, fixing her lovely big eyes fair on Dave. Poor old chap! His fork fell right out of his fingers and he did look sheepish.

"He won't sing," Sarah chimed in. "We can never get him to try, Miss Mason."

It was good of Sarah to help Dave out. Joe grinned. He always did when he was going to say something useless.

"He t-t-tried one night," he said. "The night the s-s-stallion broke out."

There was a lot of tittering. Everyone seemed to enjoy it but Bill and Dad—and Dave. Bill was studying the parson and Dad had failed to hear what Joe said. Joe lifted his voice. "I say D-Dave s-sang orright the night he f-f-frightened the s-s-stallion!"

Dad looked at Dave and "hoo-hooed". Everyone looked at Dave. Dave could feel them. He stared stolidly and stubbornly into his plate, wishing to Heaven an earthquake or something would shatter the house.

Dinner continued, but Dave couldn't eat another mouthful—and puddings and fruit and things on the table, too! He sat for a while, then, as if he had had a real good dinner, rose and left. Outside he kicked the dog for nothing at all, and went across to the thresher's tent and threw himself on a bunk. McPhee, the boss-thresher, who had knocked off early and put on his Sunday clothes in honour of "the nicht", produced a bottle from the head of his bed and asked Dave if he'd have a drop. Dave smiled and took two or three drops, and stayed all the afternoon.

At tea-time, "Call Dave," Mother said to Bill.

Bill found it hard to make Dave hear. But he came at last, came singing, "Poorsh honish parensh, born in Cashl-*hic*-maine!" Everyone listened. "No stransher he-*hic*-didsh fear"—and in the door Dave walked, looking happy. He sat at the table close to Miss Mason and smiled.

Bill began to giggle. Mother and Sarah stared at each other.

"Wheresh parshun?" Dave said, looking about the room. Joe got the giggles too. Dave grinned and closed one eye, and said to Joe, "C'n you-*hic*-shing, Miss Rudd?"

Mrs Farrell leant back, and shrieked, and held her sides.

"Where've you been?" Dad said, looking across at Dave like a Chief Justice.

"Been? 'Shup there—" And Dave spread himself out and took possession of the table. And how he did eat!

Dad finished and left abruptly, and went straight to the thresher's tent.

Mother became anxious, and went to the veranda. She was afraid of a quarrel, and stood watching. The tall green corn rustled and rasped its tangled leaves as it tossed and bent in the breeze that was springing up. Mother gave a nervous start. Dad's voice, strong and loud, floated in the air. "You did!"

"I deed-ant!"

"You did! Damn you, man, you did!"

But the row ceased suddenly. McPhee, who was a good judge of character, resorted to persuasion. He spoke softly to Dad, and patted him on the back.

"I'm frae Dumfries," he said. So was Dad.

"Yeer haun'," said McPhee.

Dad gave it, and they shook like brothers and peered affectionately into each other's eyes. Then McPhee sprung the bottle on Dad. Dad wouldn't take very much. He took about an inch.

They talked of Scotland, at least McPhee did. Dad didn't know anything about Scotland.

"No, no more," Dad said and shook his head.

"Beh! Ye're nae frae Dumfries."

"Well—just a drop, then." And Dad took some more, and smacked his lips, and said it was good stuff.

Mother remained on the veranda. As it got dark Dad came along and with him McPhee, the thresher.

The night was bright as day and a cool breeze blowing.

Mother and Sarah and Joe and the visitors sat on the veranda listening to Cook's boys, about a mile down, putting their calves in. Curlews and mopokes were about, and we could hear the possums round the corn at the seventeen-acres. Dad was inside entertaining McPhee.

Dave came out and leant against a veranda-post. "Cansh make up dansh?" he said.

"Make up a dance? Make up your bed!" Sarah answered, and Mrs Farrell shrieked again.

"D-dance, y' want?" Joe said. "Well, come on." And he seized Dave round the waist and proceeded to pull him about. They were tumbling and sprawling on the veranda like two bears when the dogs rushed out and barked. The tramp and rattle of horse hoofs, the clinging of bits and irons blended with voices, came from the rear. Next moment quite an army of mounted men and women were crowding and clamouring at the front. They yelled all sorts of friendly greetings. One, to attract attention, spurred his horse into the paling fence and swore because the animal couldn't shake an old kerosene tin off its foot. Sarah ran down the steps and hugged and kissed everything that dismounted in a riding habit.

Dave stood on the brink of the veranda and called out, "Night!"—and raised one hand, as though he would address them. Then he slipped, and fell on top of a pack of snarling dogs, and sent one yelling round the house, and made Jim Black's horse pull back and rear and mix itself up with other horses.

Dad came out and wanted to know what the devil all the row was about. Then the mob, which was a surprise party, fastened its horses to the palings and proceeded to load the veranda with provender. All were armed with eatables. Some carried them in baskets, some in bags, some in paper. Wild Dick Saunders, a rough, hairy man with a harsh, aggressive voice, who carried his in a red handkerchief, volunteered to stand guard over the pile and keep the damned dogs away.

Such a crowd! And so tall and sombre-looking at night! They tramped clumsily on the veranda and seethed and shoved like scrub cattle yarded in the moonlight.

Dad and Mother were ever so long shaking hands before they got round the lot. Long Jerry Johnson was the last, but he couldn't shake hands at all—his arms were full. He carried their baby, six weeks old, concealed in a shawl and a long dress. There the great elf stood like a dead tree, holding his offspring out from him as though it were a wet dog.

" 'Ullo! What've y' here?" Dad said. "More grub?"

"No, a ba-by," said Jerry meekly.

"A baby? Well, keep it, keep it; we don't want any o' them, do we ol' woman?"—to Mother. "We've had plenty. How many was it ol' gal—sixteen?"

"Go along!", Mother said.

"Sixteen o' 'em, Jerry! But let's see if it's like y'." And Dad grabbed the child and pushed his way in with it.

Joe grinned and whispered in Jerry's ear, "W-watch if the ol' man don't d-d-drop it. He's a bit m-merry."

Jerry jumped as if he had been struck with something. "Look out!" he said, and went through the crowd at the door like a race-horse. He asked Dad to give back the baby, but Mrs Johnson came and took the mite and put it on a bed in a back room where you couldn't hear it squeal if anyone sat on it.

The surprise party took possession of the house, bundled the tables out, hunted round for chairs and gin-cases, and set the concertina going. Then they proceeded to play games. They arranged chairs and gin-cases in a line down the room and half-way to the kitchen, and while the musician strained and jerked out a jig they pranced round until the music shut up suddenly, when they yelled and squealed and rushed headlong at the same chair, and fell on it until it collapsed and went to pieces. After that the concertina broke out again, and they picked each other out of the dust and puffed and prepared to prance more.

Wild Saunders, left in charge of the provisions, appeared at the door. "Jerry Johnson!" he shouted. "Come out here an' mind this ham-bone o' yours or the —— dogs'll have it, bag and all!"

"Oh, dear!" some said. Others went, "S-sh,"—and Miss Mason, sitting near the door, covered her ears with her hands.

But Saunders didn't apologize; he simply added, "It's a —— good job y' didn't leave the piccaninny in the bag!"

Dave sauntered in and looked round. Prompted by new-born feelings of hospitality, he went silently through the company, and, with a broad smile and no collar, shook hands with everyone, including Joe and Sarah. Then he raised himself in triumph against the wall, and struck his head hard against the shelf, and shook down the clock, and a cob of corn, and a bottle of murky looking water in which Bill, a year before, had corked a snake. The clock didn't break much, nor did the cob of corn, but the bottle containing the snake did. And the crash was hardly over when a panic set in. Such a scramble! To see them getting out both doors! And to hear them choking when they got out!

"Whatever were in the bottle?" said old Andrew O'Day in an injured tone.

Joe explained, and Andrew spat more.

"A deed horrse is naething t' it," said McPhee, walking towards his tent. And they all assembled at the foot of the steps and laughed. Inside the bottle lay silently on the floor, and the snake cast its robust fragrance upon the atmosphere in a visible cloud.

They collected the provisions and, making use of the kitchen, invited Dad and Mother and the rest of us to supper. Then all went out again and danced on the grass. And as midnight approached, and the Old Year went and the New crept in, in the shade of the sinking moon and the light of a million stars they joined hands in hearty grip and filled the corn-fields and hollow with dragging echoes of "For Auld Lang Syne".

Chapter VIII

DAVE BECOMES DISCONTENTED

ZEAL was what Dad wanted on our new selection. He told us so often. He liked to see people zealous, people who took pleasure and pride in working—for him. We could never work too hard or too long for Dad.

After dinner. Dave and Joe at the barn waiting for the horses to finish feeding. Dave sitting with his back to the slabs, his hands embracing his knees, staring thoughtfully from under an old felt hat at the stubble-field, over which a million grasshoppers sported themselves in the scorching, simmering heat. Joe lying flat on his stomach, supporting his chin in his palms, digging earth up with the toes of his boots, and dextrously spitting at ants that passed within range.

"Don't know what you think," Dave said gloomily, "but it ain't good enough for me. I've told the old chap, too, over and over again, that I won't stand it any longer. Slog away as much as y' like, an' look after things all the year, then when y' want a few bob you've to ask him for it." A pause. "An' when y' do ask he growls like a bear."

"That's so," Joe said.

"Y'd think," Dave continued, "a feller was on'y a kid, the way—"

Just then Dad appeared, using strong language to Cranky Jack for heaving a shovel at one of the mares.

"Not yoked up yet?" he growled. "Y'll take all day soon!"

"Oh, give the horses time to finish," Dave said sharply.

154

"Time t' finish!" Dad snorted. "Time for y' to yarn and idle."

Dave fixed his eyes on Dad.

"What 're y' talkin' about?" he said.

"What 'm I—damn you, feller, will y' sit there givin' impudence t' my very face? Get up, and go on with the ploughin'—the two of y'."

"Not another turn'll I do," Dave said, the tears starting into his eyes. "Not another damn stroke! Y' ain't satisfied mooching round the place all the morning, pokin' in everybody's road, but y' must come here 'n' meddle with things y' know nothing about—"

"Know nothing about?" And Dad shook with rage.

"Yes, know nothing about."

"Confound you! You insolent—" Dad was lost for a word. "Clear out of this—clear!" And up went his big right hand, after the manner of a railway guard.

"No need t' tell me," Dave said. "I've stayed here too long as it is—for all thet ever I get from y'!".

"Get from me? What the devil do you want, you hound?"

"Something more than the few miserable shillings I get once a year."

"Damn y', feller! D' y' think I'm a millionaire?"

"No—nor anyone—"

Here Mother came and intervened and tried to make peace.

But Dave was determined to leave home. He went into the house and put on a coat, then he saddled a horse and rode away. He went as far as Delaney's, five miles up.

Dad began to think, and discussed the situation with Mother.

"Well, you know," said Mother quietly, "the boys is men now, and I suppose they think that it's time they had something to themselves."

Dad thought some more, then went down to the seventeen-acres, where a man we had engaged and one of the Regan boys were pulling corn and carting it in. Dad went over their tracks and, finding a small cob with scarcely any corn on it, brought it along and threw it into the dray and lectured the man for missing it. The man offered no explanation, but young Regan grinned.

"You imp!" Dad yelled. "Get on out of that. What the devil are y' standin' for?"

The boy waded in.

Dad then lent a hand and worked hard. The dray was nearly full. The man mounted it to square the load.

"What are y' lookin' at now?" Dad shouted again to the boy, who was watching the man on the dray.

"I've finished me side," whined the boy.

"Lead the horse on, then."

"How kin I, till—"

"Lead the horse on!"

The boy ducked in time to dodge a cob Dad aimed at his head.

"You whelp!" And Dad went off round the dray after him. Regan dodged. Dad pelted more cobs at him, and roared. "Stand, you young devil, or I'll knock your head off!"

Regan gathered cobs as he ran and returned Dad's fire over the back of the horse. The man on the dray sank in a lump on the load and laughed. Regan left the dray, charged into the corn, and disappeared.

Dad threatened the man on the dray with violence and the sack, then left and went across to Cranky Jack and a traveller who was putting in a day or two for tucker. They were filling the shed with hay and must have been doing it all wrong, because as soon as Dad set eyes on it he started swearing and dancing round.

The traveller stood, holding an immense forkful of hay

above his head, and listened a second or two. Then he said, "Be damned to you!"—and threw all the hay on top of Dad, smashed the fork on the ground, heaved the pieces down the paddock, and walked off, cursing.

Dad threw the hay off himself and spat and shouted, "You coward!"

"Go 'way boss, go 'way," Jack said, "an' don't insult the gentleman. Jim's from Ireland."

Dad scowled at the half-witted man and went away. He harnessed Dave's pair of plough-horses and joined Joe.

"I'll show the feller he can be done without, I know," he said to Joe.

Joe smiled and said, "Git erp . . . Jess! . . . Jolly!" And when he stopped to clean the plough again and looked round there was Dad walloping Dave's horses with a shovel.

Joe ran back.

"What the deuce is up, n-now?" he said.

"Confound the feller!" Dad answered. "He's got the horses completely spoilt."

"They're all right," Joe said, approaching the plough-handles.

"They're not all right—they're all wrong. Stand aside, sir!" And Dad took the reins again.

"Now then!" he shouted, shaking the plough. "Get up! . . . Horses!" They jerked and swerved and shoved each other. "You damn rubbish—get up!"

"No wonder!" said Joe, making a discovery. "They're not in their right places. Put the b-black horse in the f-furrer."

"He'll go where I put him. Get up . . . you pair o' dogs! . . . Gee back . . . way! Wa-ya!" Dad dropped the plough-handles, slipped up beside the horses, and then brought the shovel down on them again so suddenly that they both bounded off before Joe could seize the reins. The next moment they were bolting across the paddock with the plough flying behind them.

Dad turned to Joe. "Dammit, why couldn't y' take the reins?"

"W-well—" and Joe grinned—"there's some things a feller can't do."

"There's a damn lot o' things y' can't do!" Dad snorted out, and went after the horses. He found them, and a portion of the plough, stuck in the fence near the barn, surrounded by Mother and Sarah and the dogs and the man who was pulling corn.

Mother wanted to know what had happened, but Dad was uncommunicative. Next day he ordered a new plough and for months afterwards the black horse hopped about on three legs.

Dave came back after tea, but scarcely looked at anyone. He rolled some clothes in a blanket, hung about for a minute or two, as though he felt sorry, then said good-bye to us all and went back to Delaney's, leaving Mother crying on the veranda.

"Mark my word," said Dad, pacing up and down, "he'll be glad to come back yet."

Dave wasn't away a week when everything was going wrong. Three cows burst on the lucerne, a mare and foal were lost, the chaff-cutter smashed in two places, and every ounce of a bullock that Dad salted went bad and was thrown out.

A hot day at Delaney's. Dave ploughing. He had scraped the plough and was standing, reflecting. He felt lonely—it was the first time he had ever been away—and couldn't help thinking of home and Mother, crying on the veranda, and of Joe and Sarah at home. "Poor old Sarah," he said aloud, when a form he knew well rode up to the fence and greeted him cheerfully.

"Hello, Dad," Dave said with a glad grin. It seemed like old times to Dave to see Dad, though it was only eight days since they had parted.

Dad dismounted and crawled through the fence.

"What's he putting in here?" he asked, surveying the ploughed land.

Dave told him. Then there was a dead silence. Even the birds and the horses' tails kept still. Dave played with some mud he had scraped from the plough, Dad with his trouser-pocket.

Dad spoke. "Better come home, Dave?" he said.

"Dunno," Dave answered, colouring up and throwing the mud down.

"This is no place for you, man—" a pause—"no place at all."

Dave gazed in silence at his boots.

"If there's anything y' want, say so, lad," Dad went on, knowing when he had an advantage.

"Here—" dragging his hand out of his pocket with a jerk —"here's a five-pound note for y' now. . . . An', goodness only knows, if ever y' want t' go t' town or anywhere y' can always take a day, or two days, or a week for that matter —can't y'?"

"Yairs . . . I s'pose s'."

"Well, come along."

Dave came. And two days later Dad called him a useless dog.

Chapter IX

DAVE IN LOVE

PLOUGHING and sowing all over. A hundred acres of the plain-land under wheat and light showers falling every week. Dad's good luck was continuing. Yet we were sharing other misfortunes freely enough. The children were all down with measles, Sarah with face-ache, Joe with a broken rib (a draught-horse broke it for him—Joe had sandy blight, and one morning approached the wrong end of a horse with the winkers), and Dave was the victim of a fatal malady.

Dave was always the unlucky one. When he wasn't bitten by a snake or a dog he was gored by a cow or something. This time it was a woman. Dave was in love. And such love! We could see it working in him like yeast. He became affable, smiled all day long and displayed remarkable activity. He didn't care how hard he worked or whose work he performed. He did anything, everything, and without help. He developed a passion for small things, trifles he had hitherto regarded with contempt, purchased silk handkerchiefs and perfume and conversation-lollies at the store, and secreted them in the pockets of his Sunday coat, which he left hanging in his room. Sarah would find them when dusting the coat and hawk them to Mother, and they'd sr nd an hour rejoicing and speculating over the discovery. Sarah never allowed any dust to settle on Dave's Sunday coat.

Dave went out every night. It amused Joe. He would be on pins and needles till supper was ready, then he'd bolt his food and rush off to saddle a horse, and we wouldn't see him again till breakfast-time next morning.

For more than a year Dave rushed off every night. "Damn! Look at that horse," Dad used to say, when he'd be at the yard. Then he'd think hard, and begin again when he met Mother. "This night work'll have t' stop, or there won't be a horse about the place fit t' ride. What the devil the fellow wants chasing round the country for every night I don't know, I'm sure." Dad knew well enough.

"Well," Mother would say good-naturedly, "you were just as bad y'self once, Father."

"Never, woman!"—with virtuous indignation. "*I* never left a horse hanging to a fence night after night to starve."

But there the matter always ended, and Dave continued his courting without interruption.

It was Fanny Bowman, of Ranger's Rise, Dave was after. She was twenty, dark, fresh-complexioned, robust and rosy, a good rider, good cook, and a most enterprising flirt.

Tom Black, Tom Bell, Joe Sibly, and Jim Moore all had sought her affections unsuccessfully. And young Cowley climbed into a loft one night and would have hanged himself with the dog-chain because of her inconstancy, only a curlew screeched "so awfully sudden" just outside the door that he rushed out and fell down sixteen steps and "injured himself internally".

Fanny Bowman was a dairymaid—mostly neat and natty and nice. But there were times when she didn't look so nice. She had frequently to go into the yard and milk fifteen and twenty cows before breakfast; and a glimpse at her then—especially in wet weather, with a man's hat on, her skirts gathered round her waist, bare-footed, slush over her ankles, slush on her arms and smeared on her face—wasn't calculated to quicken a fellow's pulse. But then it wasn't at such times that Dave passed judgment on her, any more than the city

swell would judge his Hetty while her hair was on the dresser and her teeth in a basin.

Some Sundays Dave used to bring Fanny to spend the afternoon at our place, and Jack Gore very often came with them. Jack Gore was Bowman's man, a superior young fellow, so Bowman boasted, one that could always be depended upon. He took his meals with the family and shared the society of their friends, went to church with them, worked his own horse in their plough, and was looked upon as one of the family.

Dave didn't look upon him as one of the family, though. He was the fly in Dave's ointment. Dave hated him like poison.

When it was time to leave, Dave had almost to break his neck to reach Fanny's side in time to lift her into the saddle. If he were a moment late, Gore would lift her. If he were slow at all in mounting his horse, Gore would coolly ride off with Fanny. If he didn't happen to be slow in mounting, Gore would ride on the near side of her and monopolize the conversation. He monopolized it in any case.

Mother and Sarah used to talk about Jack Gore.

"If *I* were Dave," Sarah would say, "I'm blest if I'd have her carrying on with him the way she does."

"But Fanny only means it as a sister," Mother would answer in palliation.

"Does she indeed! Dave's an old fool to bother about her at all, if y' ask me!" Sarah was developing a keen interest.

Jack Gore left Bowman's service one morning. He left it suddenly. Bowman sacked him, and Mrs Bowman talked to the neighbours about him with the wrath of an insulted mother.

"The cheek of him," she said to Mother, "to think he was good enough for Fanny! Why, we wouldn't have kept him a day if we'd thought—if we'd even dreamt. Fanny, indeed!"

But she spoke highly of Dave. She moved Mother to tears of admiration for him. And Mother couldn't resist telling Dave all that was said. Dave went to Bowman's a little earlier that night, but returned quite unexpectedly and went to bed in a bad humour.

A change came over Dave. He ceased to smile, and scarcely did any work, and never brought Fanny to see us on Sundays. At last Dave met Fanny on her way to the railway station one day, and when he came home he went straight to the album and took out her photo and jumped on it.

Jack Gore had been away from Saddletop for several months, when—"Girls are more of a trouble than boys," Mrs Bowman said despondingly to Mother one evening, at the gate. "Boys is nothing; they can always take care of theirselves. But girls—!" And she shook her head.

Jack Gore returned to Bowman's one day and neither Bowman nor Mrs Bowman attempted to chase him away. Work was suspended for twenty-four hours, and at midday,

N

a tired, dust-covered parson came to their door astride a poor horse and got down and married Jack Gore to Fanny.

It was a quiet wedding.

When they heard of it Mother and Sarah whispered things to one another, and Dad thought of Dave.

"Thank God!" he said. "The horses'll have a chance t' get fat now!"

Chapter X

WHEN DAD GOT BUCKED OFF

Mrs Talty stood at the door of her humpy looking out. She was watching Dad and Cranky Jack, on their way to the railway yards with fat pigs, about to camp for dinner in the Gap near Talty's.

Dad rode across to the humpy, got off, and asked for a billy of hot water to make tea with. Mrs Talty filled the billy, and would have handed it up when he was mounted, but Dad did not allow that—he always refused assistance in such small things. So he waved her off, and, seizing the billy, held it with the reins in his left hand. Scrambling up clumsily, he spilt the water over the mare's neck, scalded her badly, and made her buck right on to Mrs Talty. Then he fell off, and made a fool of himself.

That was how Dad happened to be in bed when a lot of people came to the house one day.

Dad was very bad, bruised all over, and the pain made him groan all day long, and whenever Mother smeared oil on him he yelled till he could be heard over at Regan's. And bad temper! If any of us poked a head into his room and asked meekly how he was, he bellowed, "Clear out!" We always obeyed. And when we didn't go in to ask how he was, he roared out to know where the devil we all were, and accused us of having no more sympathy in our compositions than a lot of blackfellows. He said we were only hanging round, waiting for him to die.

Dad was a difficult old man to please when he wasn't well.

Joe reckoned if he put the same energy into prayer that he put into profanity he would never be sick.

Nearly every female in the district called to inquire how Dad was. At least they made that their excuse. They didn't care how Dad was. It mattered little to them whether he lived or died. They came only to yarn and drink tea, and tell lies about themselves, and libel absent friends. "So sorry," they said, and made mouths and ugly faces about it. Women always make themselves ugly when they wish to appear sympathetic. It's a way they have of carrying conviction.

None ventured into the room, though, to see Dad. They questioned Mother, then sat down and sighed and took their handkerchiefs out. Fifty times and more Mother had to relate how the accident happened, and every time she came to the bucking off part Dad's voice would break through the wooden wall, "Dammit, I tell y' again I wasn't bucked off! Wasn't on the mare." And Mother would get confused, and turn all colours. And some of the ladies would smile, and some wouldn't. Then rounds of heavy groans would come from Dad, and Mother would shiver on the verge of nervous collapse lest he should break out in a passion and yell violence at the company.

Mother was unhappy. She wished the visitors had stayed away. But they didn't notice her discomfiture. They sipped tea, and ate up all the scones and cake Sarah carried in, then became boisterously convivial—screamed and took possession of the house. They forgot there was a suffering invalid on the premises, and no one heard Dad groan any more, no one heard him growl savagely, "Blast them, blast! Why the devil don't they shut up and go home?" No one but Mother. And she ran in to pacify him.

The bedlam eased off a little, and a political discussion commenced on the general election that was approaching.

Mrs Brown asked Mother whom Dad intended voting for,

and, without waiting to hear an answer, Mrs McFluster, a crane-necked, antagonistic old aunt of Mary Gray's, said her man (meaning McFluster) didn't believe in Griffith at all. In Mrs McFluster's own sinewy opinion he was of no account. She was proceeding to make remarks about him when Dad's voice fairly shook the partition. Dad believed in Griffith as he did in milk. He was Dad's political god.

Mrs McFluster pricked her ears. "What's he saying?" she asked of Mrs Higgins.

"Where the devil's there a better man for the country?" Dad shouted, his voice quivering with rage.

"Thun who?" Mrs McFluster shouted back.

"Than Griffith!" (very loud).

"McIlwraith is," squealed Mrs McFluster, "McIlwraith is, McIlwraith!"

"Never in his life! Rubbish!" Dad roared, raising himself on his elbow in the bed and glaring at the wall. "Pshaw! Y' don't know the ruffian!"

Fire flashed from Mrs McFluster's eyes as she stood up and faced the wall on the other side.

"He is, doesn't everyone know it?"

"A lie, woman; no one knows it."

Mrs Higgins and some more tugged at Mrs McFluster's skirts to induce her, in the interests of peace, to desist.

"Name me one act," Dad yelled, "one single act of McIlwraith's that was ever any good to the country. Name one, name it!"

Mrs McFluster, struggling to disengage herself from the clutches of her scared niece and Mrs Higgins, lost the thread of the argument.

Encouraged by the lady's silence, Dad got fairly on his mettle. Forgetting his bruised back, he bounded clean out of bed and grabbed his trousers.

"Name one!" he continued, yelling while he fumbled the garment excitedly.

"Name one single—" he got one leg in, and, giving the pants a tug, sprang to the door, which he opened just wide enough to disclose his face and the leg that was clothed (the rest of him was concealed)—"one single act—" fixing Mrs McFluster with a wild eye to keep her to the point "—of your McIlwraith's that was ever any good to the country. Name it!"

"The school," Mrs McFluster screeched, flying at Dad like a wild cat. "The school, the dam, the—the roads, an'—"

"Dammit, woman, they're Griffith's!" And in his excitement Dad threw open the door and stepped right out, waving his right hand (the left held up his trousers), and swinging an empty trouser-leg and displaying a huge undressed limb, all hair and joints. Sensation!

Girls squealed and jumped up and ran out in disorder.

"Father! Father!" Mother pleaded, placing her hands lightly on Dad to restrain him.

"Fanny!" Mrs Bruse called to her daughter. "Fanny, come home."

"I declare to God," Miss Mahony (a single old body, grave and religious) cried as she hurried away, "the man have no trousers on. Shame for him!"

And when she reached the door she turned and cast another glance of reprobation at Dad, then, passing the window, outside, looked in once more to satisfy herself that she wasn't doing him an injustice after all.

But Mrs McFluster saw nothing wrong. She stood up to Dad and stamped her foot and squealed out, "It's a lie! It's a lie!"—until Dave came in with a run, seized Dad in his arms and carried him back to bed.

Dad ceased yelling and calmed down, and was taking

kindly to a basin of gruel Mother brought him when someone knocked at the door again. Mother answered the call.

It was Mr Macfarlane, the minister. He smiled and
squeezed Mother's hand, then his face changed its expression.
He became solemn as a death sentence. He had heard Dad
was in a high fever, and spoke in a low anxious tone about
him. He wouldn't see Dad—he thought it well he shouldn't
be disturbed—and he suggested a short prayer for his
recovery.

Sarah came, and Mother sent her to call the boys.

"Yous fellows is wanted at the house," Dave said to Joe
and Bill, neither of whom knew the minister was there. Then
Dave, who did know, went away to close the slip-rails in
the seventeen-acres. He took till night to close those slip-
rails.

The minister was proceeding in soft, solemn tones to pray
when Dad's voice broke in upon the service.

"Ellen!" he called. Joe grinned, Mother fidgeted.

"Ellen!" he called more loudly.

"Grant them strength to bear their trial," came feelingly
from the good minister. "Where the devil've they gone t',
El-len?" came from Dad.

"Restore our dear brother to health, and—"

There was an irreverent interruption.

"Damn it!" Dad yelled, punching the partition with his
fist till it seemed the house would fall. "Damn it!"

Mother went into him.

"Where the devil've y' been?" Dad roared.

Mother motioned him to be silent, and whispered that the
minister was in the dining-room.

Dad howled harder. "Has he brought Darkey back?"
Darkey was a horse Dad had lent the parson some weeks
before.

Mother thought it wise to answer in the affirmative, and told a lie.

"Has he been feeding him?"

Mother lied again.

"Has he fetched the ten shillings he borrowed?"

"He's wandering," the minister remarked to Sarah. "They all do in fever." Then he thought he would be going and went away.

Chapter XI

DAD AND CAREY

ONE summer's night. Inside, close, suffocating, outside, calm, tranquil, not a sound, not a sign of life. The bush silent, restful. Dad on the veranda, in his easy chair, thinking; Dave, Joe and Bill stretched on the grass near the steps, dreamily watching the clustering stars.

Close to the house the eerie note of a night bird suddenly rang out. Joe and Bill turned over to locate it. Dad and Dave took no notice. The moon came slowly over the range, weird shadows fell before her and crept over the earth, and Budgee plain was a dim expanse in the hazy, languid light.

Dad spoke. "Whose stock's on Lawson's selection now?" he asked.

"Everyone's," Dave said. "Carey's, mostly."

"Well, turn everything out t'morrow that isn't ours."

Dave sat up and chuckled.

"And the Careys 'll run 'em all back," Joe joined in, "an' put ours where we'll never see 'em again."

"If they do I'll make it warm for them," Dad said.

Bill laughed.

"You wasp, get inside and don't be grinnin' like a damned cat at everythin' y' hear!"

Bill whined and said he wasn't grinning.

"Well, hold y'r noise then!" Dad shouted. Then he dragged his chair nearer the steps and spoke softly. "T'morrow that selection's mine," he said. "Lawson's thrown 't up."

Dave mounted the steps. "What, after fencin'!"

174

"After fencin'." Dad chuckled and sat back, and no more was said.

Next morning Dad repeated his instructions to Dave to turn all stock off Lawson's selection, and started for town in the sulky.

At the Lands office he was told that Lawson's selection was in the Ipswich district, and late in the day he left for home, intending to take train to Ipswich the following morning.

Dad pulled up at a wayside pub. Several men were leaning on the bar, their empty glasses before them. Dad invited them all to drink. They drank. Dad lingered awhile and chatted sociably and grew very enthusiastic about dairy farming. He exaggerated his interest and spoke of Saddletop as though he owned it all. The men became interested, one in particular. He was a Carey, and Dad in his exuberance failed to recognize him. Carey's horse had got away and he was walking home. He had twelve miles yet to tramp, and when Dad asked the company if any of them wanted work, Carey said he did. Carey knew Dad.

"Jump into the trap, then," Dad said, "an' I'll drive y' out."

Carey climbed in, and Dad drove off. All the way along he boasted of his possessions and prospects. Carey was an attentive listener and encouraged Dad to talk. Dad took a fancy to his companion, and in a lowered voice, in case some of the trees or fences concealed a pair of ears, became confidential. He revealed all he knew of Lawson's selection and his intentions regarding it, and, approaching Carey's own place, he whispered, hoarsely, "Nice set of scoundrels live there!" His companion never flinched.

"Whose place is it?" he asked.

"Carey's," Dad said, "a bad lot!" And Dad shook his head in the moonlight.

Dad pulled up at the gate.

"You camp in the barn there," he said, indicating the building with a sweep of his hand, "an' tackle the milkin' in the morning with the boys." Then Dad unharnessed the mare and went inside. The "man" went home chuckling.

Next morning Dave and Joe and Cranky Jack were in the yard milking. Dad came out.

"Where's thet feller I brought out last night—not up yet?" he asked.

Dave didn't understand. Dad explained and hobbled off to the barn. The man wasn't there. Dad returned to the yard, swearing.

"That cove wouldn't be after work," Dave drawled. "He had y'; he only wanted a lift. Plenty of his sort about."

Bill, bailing up, stood and laughed. Bill's hilarity always annoyed Dad. He chased Bill out of the yard, then roared to him to come in again. Bill slunk back.

"Go in there." Dad pointed the way through the rails. Bill hesitated sullenly. He dropped his head and turned the whites of his eyes on Dad.

"Y' hear?"

Bill moved sideways to the rails, then judged his distance and dived. But he miscalculated. His head struck the bottom rail and he rebounded, and Dad got in his kick and grinned, and forgave the man who had taken him in the night before.

Dad reached Ipswich at night and strolled about till he found a place to put up. Then he went into the streets again and gaped at things. But he didn't see many sights. There was a large store with the shutters up. The pallid light of a few flickering gas-jets revealed the outline of an old, weird weather-worn fountain, around which "the Army" crouched and yelled for the salvation of souls—and a church fence. A policeman, motionless. At regular intervals a huge clock broke the silence. It had a sad, unhealthy note, and seemed to toll a requiem for the dead. Dad stared up at it and wondered.

Morning again. Dad halted at the foot of the Lands office steps and stared in surprise. Old Carey was feeling his way down them with a stick. Carey saw Dad and grinned. Dad went into the office and came out breathing heavily. He went down the street and searched for Carey till he missed the train.

"How's it y' didn't get it?" Dave said in an unhappy kind of voice.

Dad gave no reason. He sat down and thought, and we all stood round waiting as if something was going to happen.

"They've got it all right," Dad groaned at last.

Then Dave's opportunity came. "Yairs," he said, "an' they've got all our cattle—pounded every one o' them, an' ten shillings a head damages on them."

Sarah rushed out, so did Bill and Barty; but Dave and Joe held Dad down and saved the furniture.

Chapter XII

WHEN DAD WENT TO MAREE

UP at the slip-rails Dad yarned to a man passing with
horses from New South Wales and invited him to
dinner. An interesting man, well-informed, acquainted with Tyson and Bobby Rand; knew the Queensland and
New South Wales bush through and through, and told Dad
where some good grazing land was to be selected.

Before leaving, the man sold five horses to Dad for fifty
pounds. Horses were horses then; any old sketch was worth
a five-pound note, and Dad went among the neighbours
boasting of the bargain he had made. Dad always let the
neighbours know when he had made a profitable investment;
it helped to keep their hearts up.

A brown mare among the five—by Butler, a blood horse,
the man said—turned out to be worth more than fifty
pounds herself; not to Dad, though.

Dave fed her, and raced her at Pittsworth, and was promptly taken up on the course as soon as she won.

"Stolen from old Magnus, on the Barwon," the policeman said. "Been watchin' six munch forrer."

·The other four were stolen also.

Dad cursed. Said he would never buy another —— horse as long as he lived. Then the neighbours chuckled. They always liked to remind Dad of any bad bargains he had made. It helped to keep his pride down.

Newspapers gave full accounts of the arrest of Palmer, *alias* "Whistler" Smith, on the Border.

"That's the man," Dad said. "That's the damn scoundrel —red whiskers, strapped trousers, bow-legged, finger missing —the daylight robber!" And he clenched his fists on the newspaper as though he held the delinquent in his grasp and walked up and down like a caged lion.

A constable from Toowoomba waited on Dad with a handful of legal documents and a cheque for fifteen pounds, to solicit his attendance at Maree Circuit Court as witness against Whistler Smith. He explained that the law couldn't compel Dad to cross the Border, but if he could see his way to make the sacrifice he (the Law) was certain of a conviction.

"B' heaven, then," said Dad, "I've a mind to!"

He paced about, thinking the matter out. "If y' do," the Law observed, "call on the sergeant at Goondi, and he'll fix you with a fresh horse and give you directions. An' I'd advise y', meself, to put a revolver in your pocket; it won't be any load, an' y' might want it."

"Pshaw!" Dad blurted out. "Pshaw, man! What would I be doin' with fire-arms? Haven't I travelled the country long before you were born? An' see—" Dad paused before the constable, and raising his hands, punched his own left palm hard with his right fist—"see here! An' though I'm saying it meself, never yet did I see the man—" Dad tapped his palm gently—"never yet did I see the living man—" Dad raised his right hand above his head—"I was afeared—" elevating his voice—"to take me shirt off to!" Dad pounded his palm hard.

The constable smiled and said he quite believed it.

"Well, y' better let it slide, an' stay at home," Dave said advisedly. "Y'r too old for that sort o' thing now."

Mother and Sarah, who were listening, agreed with Dave.

"Tut, tut," Dad said, "not a bit of it—not a bit of it."

Then his thoughts reverted to the fifty pounds he had lost, and an angry, vindictive spirit rose within him.

"I'll go. Policeman," he said, in a loud, decisive voice, "I'll go!" And when Dad spoke in that tone persuasion was futile.

Mounted on his old brown mare, Dad started one Friday for Maree, and how anxious Mother became the moment he disappeared from view!

Maree was three hundred miles off on the New South Wales side, and most of the track and the country were new and unknown to Dad. Yet we were sanguine enough about him. Dad had always been a wonder and an object lesson to us in the way of courage and endurance. Floods, fires, droughts—nothing ever stopped him, and for anything the bush contained in the shape of beast or being he never held a dread.

But a drought was upon the land—grass round Saddletop withered, stock poor, water scarce—and as Dad travelled on, covering mile upon mile, plain after plain, ridge after ridge, things got worse and worse. All was parched, perished; nothing but dust and desolation. The mighty bush was a vast sorrowful waste—cracked, burnt, baked. A horror? It was hell!

Shapeless, blear-eyed, loony bullocks, grotesque carica-tures, staggered pathetically by the way. All day a foul, fetid air filled his nostrils; hateful crows flocked from carcass to carcass, clamouring in fiendish exultation. And skeletons and bones lay everywhere.

At intervals Dad met pairs of grim, sullen souls along this infernal avenue, mates on the terrible track; strong, able-bodied men; men with bright, clear intellects, not loafers, not liars; British men, Australian men, shouldering their swags, almost bootless in the blistering sand, plodding through sickening, thirst-provoking heat in search of a job.

Dad left Goondi with a fresh horse, a water-bag, tucker, a head full of directions, and a revolver. The latter the sergeant had pressed on him, and Dad finally took it, saying, "Perhaps it'll be company." He carried it projecting from his coat pocket like a cob of corn.

The fourth day Dad penetrated a dense scrub, emerged on the bank of a creek, watered his horse, and, throwing the reins on the ground as with his own old mare, left him standing on the bank while he filled the water-bag. The brute made off. Dad tried to catch him, but the old moke was as knowing as a detective. He trotted when Dad ran and walked when Dad pulled up.

Dad was in a mess. Determined not to lose sight of the horse, he followed at its heels—sweating, swearing, tripping over ruts and sticks—followed till it got dark and he could see the fugitive no longer.

Weary and hungry, Dad rested at the foot of a gum-tree and thought of home and Mother and us, and called himself a darned fool, and wondered if, after all, convicting horse thieves was worth the candle.

In the morning Dad's horse was only a few hundred yards away, standing, its hind-leg fast in the bridle. Joy! Dad's heart thumped till he placed his hands on the brute and was in the saddle again. He was never so proud of a horse before. He leant over and patted it on the neck. Any other time

o

Dad would have tugged its mouth and belted its ribs.

A stifling day. The sky a great flaming oven. A hot wind blowing. Sandy, wretched, waste land to the right, the same to the left. Never a soul had Dad seen for forty miles but one solitary horseman, and he, at the sight of Dad's revolver, had galloped away.

The sun went down a ball of fire. A swamp with water and ducks in it showed itself, then off the road a public-house, a dusty, tumble-down old rookery. A couple of saddle-horses outside, fastened to trees. Four persons lounged on the veranda, two with beards, strapped trousers, and spurs, the other two scarcely more than youths, one a half-caste.

"G' day," Dad said.

" 'Day."

And when Dad dismounted every eye there was on his horse.

Behind the bar, hurriedly scrubbing a glass with a dirty towel in anticipation of trade, stood a lame, one-eyed warrior with scars on his head.

Dad called for a beer, then glanced back at the horse. Dad remembered the sergeant's warning. Dad took the beer and drank it at the door.

"Come far?" the publican said, eyeing Dad closely.

"Two hundred and fifty miles, I dare say," Dad answered.

"Queensland?"

Dad was wondering whether he would answer or not when a horseman of the flash bush type reined up at the door. He spoke to those outside, then called out, "Riley!"

Riley crept under the counter and limped to the door.

"The traps passed Bingiloo yesterday with the Queenslander," the horseman shouted.

Riley didn't understand. "With who?" he asked.

"The witness to fix Whistler; they're fetchin' him in irons."

The half-caste sniggered ironically. Riley looked grave.

Dad stepped out, and, clearing his throat, fixed the man on horseback with both eyes. "It's a damn lie!" he roared.

Every eye was upon Dad in an instant. For a moment a dead silence. Dad squared himself and stood up to it, hasty, haughty-looking.

"It's a damn lie!" he roared again. "F'r I'm the man, an' where 're me irons?" He stepped aside, displaying his big feet for inspection.

The horseman scowled, but something he read in a glance from Riley changed his expression.

He dismounted and approached Dad, smiling. "You're Mr Rudd, then," he said, "from the head of the Condamine?"

"I am," Dad answered, never changing a muscle. The man said he had been to Dad's several times. He spoke well of it and told Dad he was a nephew of old Gray's.

Dad forgot the sergeant's warning. He seized Gray's "nephew" by the hand and shook it.

"Well, well," he said, "an' I took y' for a horse stealer." And Dad chuckled by way of apology. Gray's "nephew" chuckled also.

The publican proposed a drink. Dad drank and returned the shout. That was at seven o'clock.

Midnight. The moon shone fitfully and lit up the belt of cabbage gums; from the swamp came the trumpet note of wild geese; owls on noiseless wing were hunting round; a dim, sickly light flickered at the pub. Two horsemen rode away from it through the trees, leading a horse with a saddle on. From a back room a voice kept calling, "Dorgsh! Robbersh! P-ubli'an! P-ubli'an, wher'sh me-*hic*-r'holver?"

The voice was Dad's.

The principal witness for the Crown failed to attend, and the case against Palmer, *alias* Smith, broke down.

183

Chapter XIII

THE NEW TEACHER

VERILY, Saddletop was going ahead. A new church and an old public-house went up, the public-house that used to be at the Gap. A camp of men came along with a tent and some tools, and dug a new government dam; some more cleared the lanes of timber and trees, felled them and chopped them up and left them stacked in heaps on the roadway to frighten horses and make them bolt.

A lot of new selectors came and brought large families with them and murmured like the Israelites because the school was six miles from them. Dad became their Moses.

He couldn't see what they had to grumble about, but Dad always listened to people with a grievance. He went to work and agitated earnestly for a new school at our end of the district. Dad worked night and day to get them that school, and when at last it was granted and the building went up they murmured more because it was erected within a few feet of Dad's land.

One day, a young man, overwhelmed with a collar—a lean stripling of a man, with no more hip than a goanna, a clean face, a "haw" in his voice, a cane in his hand, and a gorgeous band on his straw hat—mounted the veranda and announced himself to Dad as the teacher of the new school.

Dad scarcely heard him. He was confused. He stared and couldn't think of anything to say. Had the Angel Gabriel, or the hangman, suddenly appeared before him, Dad's equanimity couldn't have been more disturbed. Dad was never himself in the presence of leading people, and the prig-pedagogue and the sage were one and the same to him.

The teacher bowed and said he believed Dad was Mr Rudd. His own name was Wood-Smyth—Mr Philip Wood-Smyth—and he handed Dad a card, and, sitting in an easy chair, began to talk of schools and curriculum in an earnest and learned manner. He believed in teaching a boy mathematics, and mentioned Napoleon Bonaparte and others whom Dad hadn't heard of, but he condemned classics and the dead languages.

"What is the use of them?" he said. "What earthly use is Greek to you now on this farm, Mr Rudd?" Dad looked along the veranda boards. "Can you say you have ever found your Latin or your ethical problems in Shakespeare of any use to you since you left school?"

Dad, in tones of uneasiness, said he hadn't.

"And yet—"

Mother found her way to the veranda and Dad told the

teacher she was Mrs Rudd. They shook hands, and when Mr Wood-Smyth looked round to address Dad again he was gone.

The new teacher was a polite man and enjoyed society. Never before had there been anyone like him at Saddletop. Whenever he met Miss Wilkins or Gray's daughters or Sarah he would smile and take off his hat and strike his knees with it. And it didn't matter how far off they were, whether on a veranda a mile away or on horseback or carrying in sticks, he smiled and took his hat off just the same.

Dave regarded Mr Wood-Smyth with disfavour. The polish of him and his attention to girls annoyed Dave.

"He's a goat, no matter how much he knows," Dave said in the kitchen one day.

Sarah stood up for the ways of the pedagogue. She thought it proper such respect should be shown to her sex.

"Then you're mighty fond o' being noticed," Dave answered cynically.

Young Bill was sitting at the table, having late dinner alone. He joined in.

"Not when they're m-milkin', Dave, an' haven't their stockin's on—" Dave looked at him and grinned—"or 'n a tub."

Bill struggled on the floor from a poke Mother gave him with the teapot.

"But it wouldn't hurt you," Sarah went on quietly, "to lift your hat."

"No, it wouldn't," Dave snarled, "an' it wouldn't hurt anyone if I didn't. An' who wants t' wear a hat out swingin' it about as if he wanted t' block a cow?" And Dave chuckled triumphantly and went out.

Mr Wood-Smyth was a frequent visitor at our place, and if he chanced to remain for a meal any time Dad would become agitated. He would lose his head and at the table

186

make all kinds of mistakes. When he didn't pass meat to someone who didn't want any, he dropped the plate and spilt gravy about or mutilated his fingers with the carver.

But Dad usually contrived to avoid Wood-Smyth's society. Dad had never received a great education himself, and the presence of so much learning annoyed him. But always when the teacher had left Dad talked favourably of him. Once Mother asked how much salary he thought Mr Wood-Smyth received, and Dad reckoned he would get at least a thousand.

Politeness was the broad plank in Wood-Smyth's curriculum and he hammered it hard into his pupils.

One day Dad was riding on the road and met the scholars returning home. Several raised their hats to him. Dad stared and went on. Some more hats. Dad scowled. Then Tom limped along, swinging a lizard by the tail.

"Hello, Dad." And up went his hat.

Dad turned the mare sharply and went after him.

"Y'r young devil!" he shouted, striking at Tom round the base of a tree with a riding-switch. "Would y' make sport o' me, too?"

" 'E tol' us t'—" Tom whined:

"Who?"

"S-S-Smith."

"T' make fun o' me?"

"No, t'—"

Dad attempted to dismount and Tom dropped the lizard and escaped.

Boxing Night. A party at our place—Sarah's party. Such a gathering! Every soul on Saddletop must have been present—everyone except the Careys. And the display of lights and lanterns would have almost blinded you. The verandas right round were hung thick with them. Two accordion players and a violinist were in attendance, and to hear the music they made when you reached the gate would make your heart jump.

Sarah flew about everywhere, met her female friends at the steps and hugged them, and escorted them in and took their hats and things and found sleeping places for the babies.

Joe looked after the men for her, warned them of the dog and the barbed wire, showed them where to put their horses, and conducted them to the ballroom and introduced them to any young ladies they didn't know.

Dancing about to commence. Mr Wood-Smyth arrived. He came late and McGregor, a very old mate of Dad's, strolled in about the same time. Dad hurried forward and seized McGregor by the hand and welcomed him boisterously. Dad hadn't seen McGregor for a number of years and the pair sat together at a table and talked of old times. They talked for hours.

Intermission. The room containing Dad and McGregor became crowded and cake and coffee were being handed round.

A lull in the clatter of tongues. McGregor turned to Mr Wood-Smyth, who sat near him sipping coffee, and in a loud sonorous tone said, "N' hoo's th' auld mon—quite weel, Phil?"

Dad stared and nudged McGregor. He thought his old mate was making a mistake.

But Wood-Smyth understood. He blushed and fidgeted, then forced a smile and answered, "He's—ah—pretty well, indeed."

"An' auld Mick?"

Mr Wood-Smyth fidgeted more. He wished someone would come to the door and call him. The company appeared interested.

"Pretty well, I think," he said, eyeing the door.

McGregor turned to Dad. "Y' ken auld Micky,"

McGregor said, "who cleanit the dustboxes i' Dreeyton—
uncle to this mon?" And he pointed his thumb at the teacher.

Dad drew himself up like a cockatoo, aroused. "Not his
uncle!" he exclaimed, his eyes opening like a door.

"Yes, mon—" and McGregor laughed at Dad's astonished
look—"yes, Phil's a son o' auld Jem Smith, o' Quartpot, is
he nae? An' wus nae auld Micky a brither o' Jem's?"

The discovery was too much for Dad. He stood up and
stared at Wood-Smyth.

"Dammit!" he said. "I know y'."

"Y' couldna f'get auld Jemmy." McGregor said.

"Remember him well," Dad answered, his eyes shining
with enthusiasm. And turning to the company, who, to the
discomfort of the teacher, were all grinning, he said, with
a ring of pride in his voice, "His father an' me knew one
another thirty year ago."

"Eh! An' th' auld woman tae," said McGregor.

"An' his mother," Dad answered.

"An' y' min' th' bannocks she used tae mak' us a'?"

Dad burst into a loud laugh at mention of the bannocks.
But Wood-Smyth didn't. He only smiled, but his face was
very red.

"An' min', too, th' auld black hen she used to hae sittin'
wi' eggs in the bed?"

Dad held his sides, and the tears ran down his furrowed
cheeks.

"An' the p-p-p—" McGregor couldn't speak for laughing—
"the pig i' the hoose wi'—" choked again—"wi' ribbon tied
tae it!"

Dad gave a tremendous roar. The whole house exploded,
and it was minutes before Joe's voice could be heard yelling,
"S'lect your partners for a waltz."

Chapter XIV

THE PRODIGAL'S RETURN

I N harvest time. Dave and Joe and Bill carting barley off
the house-paddock. Dad poking round on his old mare
annoying the cows.

Dave, in the act of heaving a sheaf into the dray, paused
and looked up, "Who's the cove?" he said wonderingly. Joe,
from the top of the load, stared in the direction of the
house. Bill, on the opposite side to Dave, walked round and
took observations. Bill, always dog-tired, never lost an
opportunity to recover.

"Dunno," Joe said. "They're all shakin' his hand, anyway."

"Another parson, I s'pose," Dave groaned apprehensively.
Dave disliked the clergy. Their presence always made him
unhappy, and one of them in the house would almost drive
him from home. And parsons were never in any hurry to
leave our place now. Different from Shingle Hut. It was
rarely that they remained there for a meal; never when
there was a well-butchered leg of a kangaroo hanging under
the veranda. Dad mostly saw that one was dangling there
whenever a parson was reckoned to be due. And he would
tear it down and heave it into the grass the moment the
pilot had left. Dad was a wise man, though he is not mentioned in Proverbs.

"His nag's poor enough for a parson's," Joe chuckled,
"on'y y' never see 'em with two—one's always dead 'fore
they get another."

Bill laughed a stiff, ready-made laugh to encourage the

conversation and prolong the "recovery". But Dave wired in with the fork in silence.

To gain time Bill asked Dave a useless question. He said, " 'Ow'd yer like t' be a parson, Dave?"

Had it been anyone else Dave might have committed some violence. But he always got on well with Bill. He only turned his eyes on him in forgiveness.

The stranger, wagging his head and working his hands and arms like a temperance orator, was walking between Mother and Sarah, both hatless and holding newspapers above their heads, towards the house. They seemed to know him, and listened eagerly to things he had to say.

Joe couldn't make him out. Bill volunteered to run up and see what he was. Then Joe grinned. He remembered when he had been like Bill.

The stranger tossed a greasy bundle he had taken from his saddle on to the veranda, and the next moment was striding over the stubble towards the dray. He carried his head high, his hat well back, and walked like a person not afraid of trespassing.

"I know that stride," Dave said thoughtfully and stared hard.

The man drew near. His hair and whiskers were long and wild, and running to seed. Bill giggled and stared. Dave stood thinking of that stride.

In the tongue of the cheerful aboriginal the man called out things as he approached. Joe didn't understand, but he disapproved of them and yelled back, "Get y'r 'air cut!" Bill sniggered and, crouching down, took the pitch-fork with him under the dray. But Dave suddenly cast his away.

"Bless me! It's Dan!" he exclaimed, and damaged several barley stooks tumbling over them to reach him.

Bill crawled out from under the dray without the pitch-fork and rolled his eyes about. Joe slid off the top and tore his trousers and dragged half the load down on top of himself.

"Dan," each murmured, following Dave.

Dan it was. The same old Dan that Dad had twice hunted from home, but older, shabbier, more useless, and more dilapidated.

He shook Dave's hand with fervour, but he didn't know Joe from Bill or Bill from Joe till Dave mentioned their names. Bill looked pleased. He felt proud of Dan. Often he had heard of him; he used to wonder if he would ever see him; and now all at once Dan stood before him. And as Dan proceeded rapidly to account for fourteen years of absence, Bill stared him all over, and hugged the ground near his careless, greasy form.

Almost before you could think, Dan had plunged into the back country; fought several fights with naked blacks; dashed into a scrub in pursuit of brumbies on a horse called Silver Star, coming out without a stitch on but his boots and belt; had broken his right leg three times in the same place; lost three hundred pounds on the Cooper, and was rejoicing on his way to Sydney in charge of a thousand wild C.O.B. bullocks.

Bill's breath threatened to leave him. His mind wasn't nearly large enough to hold the impressions Dan made on it. Even Joe—Joe who was always cool enough to calculate —was carried away, and a lively longing to see some outback life filled his soul. But Dave was only moved to a smile. Dave remembered Dan.

"Let's go up to the house," Dave said, and as they all walked on Dan continued. "I've seen life! Fancy humpin' a swag from Nudgee Nudgee to Normanton—five hundred miles—without a boot on or a bob about y', and the last stage havin' t' pull off and fight two infernal big Danes fer three hours fer your own water-bag. An'—" pausing to breathe —"after knockin' 'em both out, t' have t' pour every drop o' water down their blanky throats t' bring 'em round!"

A thrill of excitement went through Bill. He swung his clenched fist at the imaginary forms of the Danes and caught Dave in the small of the neck.

"Damn y'!" Dave yelled. "Damn y'!" And he sprang on Bill, and squeezed his neck, and there must have been trouble only Bill managed to gasp that he "didn't m-mean t' ".

They reached the house just as Dad arrived at the steps on the mare.

"Don't! See if he knows me," Dan said, silencing Bill, who began yelling to announce the home-coming of the heir.

Dad stared hard from the party approaching him to the horses left unprotected in the dray, scowled, and looked ugly.

Dan separated himself from the others.

"Doesn't know me from a crow—told y' he wouldn't," he said, saluting Dad as though Dad were a colonel with gold lace and a wooden leg.

"I don't know who y' are, man," Dad answered gruffly and was about to revile Dave for wasting time when Dan bowed like a man winding water and said, "Your fust-born . . . Daniel, sir—Daniel Damascus Rudd."

Dad nearly fell off the mare.

"Dan!" he blurted out and urged the old mare towards the prodigal and stretched out his hand. But all at once he checked himself. He remembered he had kicked Dan out and never wanted to see him again. He changed colour.

Then it was that Dan showed himself a strategist.

"Not a word—not one syllable," he said in grave tones, seizing Dad's hand without a blush. "I know what's in your mind, exactly. Say nothing—it's past. Let it slide. . . . You turned me out, that's true, but I don't mind—I deserved it. But I went—I obeyed like a man, didn't I? And now—" Dan paused, so that Mother and all standing round might hear—

"and now I'm back—" paused again—"back a wiser—" another pause—"a better—" here Dan smote himself hard on the thigh where his pocket had been, before he tore it out to wear on his foot—"and—" elevating his voice—"a richer man—wanting no one's favour, fearing nobody's frown!"

Dan was a rare speaker.

Dad never before displayed so much agility in dismounting, except when he fell off. He gripped Dan by both hands. Large tears like hailstones gathered and broke in his big eyes, and one smothered sob like a colt choking was all we heard. It was too much for us. We stared at our feet and felt we should have been dead. If there was one thing more than another we couldn't stand it was Dad blubbering.

"Never mind," Dan said in tones of forgiveness, holding a hand high above Dad's head. "Never mind! Fer me own part it's fergotten long enough ago, 'n' I'm back. 'N', as I hinted before, well off, Dad, well off—independent!" And he looked down on Dad and smiled.

Dan was an object lesson in filial affection.

Dave smiled, too, and went back to work. Dave smiled because he knew what a beautiful liar Dan was.

Dan followed Dad inside and had something to eat. He ate everything Sarah placed before him. Then he sat back, and all the rest of the afternoon talked to Dad and Mother, and admired the furniture, and smoked and spat. But he didn't spit on the floor. He rose every time and went to the door and did it on the clean boards of the veranda that had just been scrubbed.

Dan confided to Dad his plans for the future. He'd had enough outback life, he said, and intended putting a bit of money into a farm and settling down. If he could get a suitable place, about eighteen hundred acres with water, he'd start dairying, milk a hundred cows, feed them on lucerne, and fatten wethers and steers beside.

Dad said there was a big thing in it, and knew the very place Dan required—"Curry's," he said, "joining me. Two thousand acres, creek runnin' right through it, two pounds ten an acre."

"We'll have a look at it," Dan said reflectively.

Just before tea-time Dan apologized to Mother for the sad condition of his clothes. "Fact is," he remarked, "me wardrobe's comin' down be train, so I'm afraid y'll have to put up with me as I am till it's here."

Mother said if he liked he could put on some of Dave's for a change. Dan thought he would. He put on a full suit of Dave's, besides a shirt and collar, and came to tea a new man. He put them all on the next day, too, and never took them off any more.

For nearly a month Dad accompanied Dan through the district, inspecting farms that were for sale, and at night they would sit together on the veranda and discuss the advantages and disadvantages of each. And when Dad would advise Dan to buy a certain one, Dan would disagree and express a preference for some other, always concluding with "Better t' wait a bit yet, 'fore decidin'." In the morning Dad would have to go to work, but Dan preferred to sit on the veranda smoking, and making up his mind.

Dan was going to give five pounds to a young lady who called one day collecting for the hospital, but all his money was in the Savings Bank and he hadn't any change about him. "Worst of banks," he said, "can't run to them when y' wants to."

But Mother had plenty in the house and offered him the sum till he could draw some of his wealth. Dan accepted it and went to the veranda and gave the young lady a half-sovereign he had found in Dave's trouser-pocket.

"Alwez like t' give t' the hospital," he said, returning to

Mother. "Altergether, I s'pose I've given hundreds o' pounds, now."

Mother was delighted with the way Dan had turned out and was anxious to know the property he meant to buy. She questioned Dad about it one morning.

"I don't know," Dad said angrily, "I don't know what the devil he's going t' do."

Dad began to treat Dan badly again. He showed feelings of distrust towards him and refused to accompany him any more to inspect properties. Dan took offence. He went away one morning to buy Curry's place, and when we heard of him again he was working among the selectors at McCatta's Corner, about eight miles away.

Dan never bought any farm, but he settled down. He married Mary MacSmith—had a great wedding, too—and lived comfortably and happily on his wife's people. And he promised to do well, till one day, about three months after his marriage, Mrs Geraghty dragged her daughter Polly, who was crying, into MacSmith's place, and, within hearing of the whole family, told Dan he wasn't a man or he would have married Polly, and asked him what he meant to do.

Dan was imperturbable. He laughed and said, "Git out!"— and would have argued himself innocent, but his wife, the very person you'd expect to stand up and fight for him and decline to hear anything the MacSmiths would say, believed it all and flew into tears and hysterics, and Dan, of course, was thrown on the cold world again.

In compensation for Dan's infidelity, his wife rushed to the store and got a cart-load of goods in his name. Dan got the bill. It made him restless. He came to Dave for advice. Dave read the bill and when he saw the last item looked up and asked, "What did she want with twenty-four pair o' stockin's?"

"Dunno," Dan said. "She must be a blessed centerpee'!"